for Mary
my guiding star

THE CALL

a virtual parable

PAT RUSHIN

POD Edition, 2020.
ISBN: 978-1-941681-04-6

Book Design by Tina Craig
Cover Art by Plinio Marcos Pinto
Title Page Illustration by Terry Gilliam

Acknowledgements
The Call was the winner of the 2009 Blodgett Waxwing Literary
Prize awarded by *The King's English*. Parts of *The Call* appeared, in
a different form, in *Zoetrope All-Story*. Prior to publication, *The Call*
was adapted for film by the author and became *The Zero Theorem*,
directed by Terry Gilliam.

null-com

The phone rings. We answer. "Hello?" we say, and we say this hopefully, hoping beyond hope that this call is the call we've been waiting for all our lives. We listen. "Fine," we say, "and you?" We listen further. "Oh," we say, "no," we say, "we live in an efficiency apartment, and we doubt that Management would authorize the sort of installation you wish to install. However, although we are frankly disappointed by the nature of your call, we thank you just the same for calling."

We take our dinner out of the freezer. We are not at all interested in our dinner, but we have chosen to prepare and eat it nonetheless. We place our dinner in our microwave oven and set the timer. We lay out dishware, glassware, cutlery, and disposable paper napkin on our galley kitchen countertop. We stare at our galley kitchen wall where a window might be were we not ensconced in a discounted interior unit, idly tintinnabulating our fingers on the stainless steel kitchen sink. Our view neither inspires nor deflates us.

The phone rings.

The microwave beeps.

We suffer a moment's quandary before we pick up our phone, which is portable, and answer it on our way to the microwave oven. "Fine," we say, spooning our microwaved dinner from its microwavable container onto our dishware, "and you? Oh," we say, "no," we say, "we are not at all interested. Yes," we say, forking a forkful of dinner into our mouth, "you have indeed caught us at an inconvenient time. We were just eating our dinner. We are, in fact, continuing to eat our dinner even as we speak around it, and will presently continue continuing to eat our dinner. Our dinner does not especially please us, but we are presently watching our weight—at present, we meant to say—" we say, "and we understand that weight watching requires the regular intake of calorically monitored meals, especially pleasing or not... No," we say, "there is perhaps no better time for you to call, since the past is finished, the future remains a cipher, and the present presently continues to be as inconvenient as it was when first you called, now some time past."

The phone beeps.

"Excuse us momentarily for a moment," we say. "We subscribe to a Call Waiting service, and an irritating beep audible only to ourselves has signaled another caller's call waiting for our answer. Coincidentally, we ourselves have been waiting for a certain call all our lives, and the caller waiting for us to answer may, in fact, be the source of that call. We have some hope," we say, "so that we must presently—and we do mean presently at present—push our flash button which will consequently put your call on Call Waiting and connect us with our Call Waiting caller's call. Of course, you're familiar with the technology," we say. "We intended no condescension. One moment, please."

We press flash.

"Hello?" we say, hopeful yet understandably wary. "Yes, this is we," we say, wary yet unable to resist wading through the shallow puddle of hope shimmering in our heart. "We have felt finer in the past," we sigh, resigned, "and in that past we may have expressed more civil concern in return for how you are feeling this evening yourself, but at present we are trying to eat our dinner, a dinner which, with its thickly ichorous consistency whose flavor defies definitive describability, we are not especially pleased by. By which we are not especially pleased, we meant to say," we say. "But a dinner which needs to be eaten nonetheless. We should also mention that we interrupted a previous call to answer your Call Waiting call, hoping beyond hope that yours might be the call we have waited—"

We find ourselves interrupted.

"We understand that you have a job to do," we say, "since we ourselves are employed and have our jobs to do each day as well. We are a cruncher of entities by profession, and, occasionally, as we crunch our various entities, we find ourselves growing a tad impatient, and we see our entities as nonsensical units of no inherent value, but yet and still and all—"

We find ourselves interrupted again.

"It has become apparent to us that you consider the making of your livelihood more crucial than the objections we might raise to your making your livelihood at our disinterested expense while a caller on Call Waiting awaits—"

We find ourselves interrupted a third and final time.

We press flash.

"Hello?" we say, and we hang up.

We finish our dinner. Our dinner, in the final analysis, has neither pleased nor especially displeased us. We wash and towel dry our dishware, cutlery, and galley kitchen countertop. We enter the main room of our one-room efficiency and ease ourselves into the swiveling easy chair in front of our computer work station. We find a certain irresistible logic in this move.

The phone rings.

We eye the phone quandawarily. We have been waiting for a call all our lives, and, although the nature of the call we have been waiting all our lives for, for which we've been waiting all our lives, remains by its very nature both essentially and quintessentially a mystery to us, we cannot help but hope that said call will somehow change our lives in indescribably delicious ways. And yet, still swiveling uneasily in our easy chair, we find that hope metaphorically dampening, so that we decide to let the phone ring. The phone stops ringing, we sigh with a mixture of regret and resigned relief, and the phone begins ringing again.

We are beginning to perceive a pattern here. We have perceived patterns previously in our lives, and we have adjusted our paradigms accordingly to fit the parameters of the several patterns we've perceived.

We rise from our chair, go to our tool drawer, withdraw and reject a variety of tools. Screwdrivers, both straight slot and Phillips-head. Pliers, needle-nose and channel-lock. Wrenches, socket and box, crescent, metric, and standard. Finally we select a tool we've never found a use for, our ball-peen hammer, a former anniversary present from one of our ex-spouses. We heft it by its handle, feel its reassuring weight cantilevering in our tightening grip. Patiently, expertly, and not precisely without a certain measure of joyful dissatisfaction, we smash the phone until the ringing stops. We continue smashing for a time thereafter.

We work up a sweat.

•

Our intercom buzzes. We rise from our computer and answer. "Phoneman," a burly voice announces. "Management says you got a problem."

"No problem," we say. "We fixed it ourselves."

"Management says take a look. Let me up, man."

We buzz the ground floor door and open our apartment to the kind of massively swarthy and hirsute brute who, in our previous lives, might have wooed several of our eventual ex-spouses into trembling acts of sweaty intromission, grunting emission, languid remission, and unhealthy inhalation of a shared filtered cigarette.

"*Hell*-o," phoneman says, glancing at the shattered plastic on our galley kitchen countertop. "You do this all by yourself?"

"Selves," we amend. "We were having trouble with our phone. We endeavored to ameliorate the problem."

"Using this?" Phoneman picks up our ball-peen hammer by its head, pokes at the phone rubble with its shaft. "Not the proper tool, sir, if you don't mind a word of constructive criticism." Phoneman shakes his shaggy head. "Your ball-peen's used for hammering out dents and dimples in sheet metal. Fender-bender on the old jalopy, say. In a pinch you can hammer a nail with a ball-peen, though I wouldn't recommend it. An acceptable third use, depending on your strength and temperament, is as a personal security device, the hemispherical peen end leaving a dandy dent in the skull of even the most hardheaded of your garden variety antagonists. Concussion. Bleeding from the ears. A loud knock at death's door. But the ball-peen is *not* your tool of choice for a close-tolerance job like fixing phones."

Phoneman frowns, wags his shaggy head, hammer gripped tight in his sweaty hand. "If I may speak candidly, sir..."

We shrug. We have no feelings one way or the other.

"People like you, people who don't show sufficient respect for protocol to select the proper tool for the proper job, those kind of people make me sick."

"Then leave us," we say.

"Who's us?"

"We, ourselves."

"But there's only the one of you."

"So it would appear. Allow us to show you the door."

"Not until I've done my job."

"We won't pay for your services."

"Management's paying. They'll bill your security deposit. You're extraneous, except as a buzzer-upper of service callers. Try to keep yourselves out of my way and let me work."

He hunkers in front of the phone, poking and prodding, muttering.

"Unfixable," he proclaims finally. "I'll have to hook up a new one, soon as I rewire the jack you thoroughly took the business end of the wrong tool to."

"To which we thoroughly took etcetera," we say. "You dangled your preposition."

"Dangle this," phoneman says, grabbing his crotch. "What's wrong with people like you who destroy beautiful circuitry, correct my grammar, and make me sick?"

"We subscribe to your company's Call Waiting service," we explain. "We have been waiting for a call all our lives. Your service did not provide that call. Instead, it provided a host of other callers access to our initially hopeful yet increasingly more impatient ear. We could no longer stand the ringing, ringing, ringing of the bells bells bells bells bells bells bells. We schized."

"That explains a lot," phoneman says. "I wish people like you would explain themselves to people like me more often. Now I understand, so now I can help you."

We breathe a sigh of not completely credulous relief.

"Once upon a time, the system was the solution," phoneman goes on. "That's no longer true—not since the D-d-d-d-divestiture—I generally tell people like you not to flush the diaper with the doo-doo. The system is certainly still a preferable *alternative* to the more radical solution of hammering your phone to smithereens. I can fix you up pronto. Wait a sec while I visit my van."

We wait considerably more than a sec but spend those excess secs fruitfully crunching entities at our computer.

"Here we go," phoneman says when we buzz him up to install our shiny new and, he promises, improved phone system that will make it possible for us to communicate without ever having to answer the phone again. "Voice mail," he says, "custom tailored to satisfy the special individualized needs of people like you. We can program it now if you like."

We like.

Phoneman produces a clipboarded survey and spends the next several hours asking us highly personal questions concerning our past and present lives. We answer as truthfully as is humanly possible. Finally, phoneman goes to work programming, and before we know it he has personally set up our new Call Filtering system.

"Your main line screens your calls through Caller ID, matching the caller's origination number against the digitally updatable list of numbers you've provided, and routing known numbers each to its proper voice mailbox. Let's test it. I'm really eager to show off. Say one of the ex-spouses you referred to calls."

He pushes a series of numbers on a hand-held receiver hooked between our wall jack and telephone. "Thank you for calling," a digitally officious recorded voice announces:

> *If you have not received our monthly check, be assured that we either have or will have posted it by mail in time to reach you within strict court-sanctioned time constraints.*

"Or suppose one of your many children calls," phoneman says.

> *Thank you for calling. We love you and are proud of you and are here for you at the sound of the beep and will get back to you at our earliest convenience. We love and miss you so. Don't for a moment believe what your mothers claim with regard to us.*

"With similar specialized lines for business calls…"

"We don't do business by telephone."

"Just the same, you have the option. Another line for friends and acquaintances…"

"Not a burning need."

"Still an option. You never know when some old school chum, drunk late at night and tripping down Memory Lane with the old yearbook, might try to disturb your sober slumber… And my personal favorite, the Phone Solicitation Courtesy Acknowledgment Mailbox Loop #67, which thanks your so-called Courtesy Callers for calling and directs them to press 6 to reach you, with 6's message thanking them again for calling and directing them to press 7 to reach you, with 7's message once again thanking them for calling and directing them to press 6 to reach you, leaving them at sixes and sevens, a stroke of genius I plan to file a patent on just as soon as I leave here."

"Test the mailbox for the call we've been waiting all our lives for."

Phoneman grimaces, punches buttons.

> *This is we. If your call does not fit into one of the voice mailboxes previously listed, your call may be the call we have been waiting for all our lives. For which we have been waiting etc. If so, please stay on the line, and we will answer at the very first ring.*

"Perfect," we say.

"If it makes you happy."

We withdraw a credit card from our wallet. "How much do we owe?"

"Put that away!" phoneman barks. "Never, *ever*, show *anybody* your credit cards. People can conjure with them."

We put our wallet away.

"Besides, I told you," phoneman says, slouching shaggily to the door. "I only deal with Management." He touches the doorknob, hesitates. "Are you by any chance albino?"

"No."

"Then if you don't mind some constructive criticism," he says, opening the door, "you really should think of getting out more. Any problems, give me a call."

And with that he's gone, leaving us blissfully alone.

tele-lude

The phone doesn't ring. We call.

"I was afraid of that," phoneman says. "Feast or famine. From too many calls to none at all. I'm guessing from your whiny tone you're dissatisfied."

"We are satisfied that we no longer receive calls from phone solicitors and ex-spouses," we explain, "and we can live with the fact that our children generally refuse to call, let alone leave messages, aside from a single exception assuring us that it will be, and we paraphrase, a chilly day south of Purgatory before he or she digits his or her way through our baroque voice-mail menu to request an audience with an expletive-deleted machine, end of paraphrase."

"Sharper than a fucking serpent's tooth. Sad, really. But you can take some comfort in the fact that this child was actually speaking to a voicemail simulacrum of you and not to you yourself."

"As we've said, we can live with such non-calls, as we can live with the non-calls of telemarketers and the non-calls of our many non-friends. However, we *still* have yet to receive a call from the caller whose call we have waited all our lives for."

"Fill me in again?"

"The call we feel assured will change our lives in indescribably delicious ways."

"Oh. Yes. That call. I had my doubts all along."

"Can you help us further?"

"Afraid not," phoneman says. "I'm not a phoneman anymore. I'm an entrepreneur now. I patented that 67 Loop, made a bundle, and served notice as of today. I should thank you. I *do* thank you. And I will thank you further by putting in a call to a person I know who shoots trouble for a living. Will you be home today?"

"All day, every day, as usual," we say.

web-com

Troubleshooter," a coy and lilting voice assures us when we press our buzzing intercom's button. "Buzz me up, babe... Oh!" she continues, drawing back a step when we open our apartment door. "What's with you, poor sofa spud, hanging all void and shroomy?"

"Phoneman says we need to get out more."

"The phoneman knows phones," she says, brushing languidly past us. "I know getting out more. Definitely overrated. But one person's bit is another's byte, as they say... My," she exclaims, appraising our apartment's interior, "I never knew they made efficiencies so eensy-meensy-weensy. Cute, but hardly big enough for Barbie, let alone Ken and Skipper too. You're staring at me. Why are you staring at me?"

Dressed all in white from top of deeply-plunging neckline to tip of high-riding hem (revealing tops of gartered white stockings below), she sports the sort of long-legged, high-breasted, tightly-clad, nursely-pure beauty that would have enticed us in our earlier years to actively woo, optimistically wed, and boldly impregnate her, tossing all cautionary thought of inevitable divorce and debilitating alimony to the wind—the wind that, had we a window in our apartment, would now be caressing her snow-white mane's lascivious curls at this very moment, were it—the window—opened.

At times like these, we can barely stand to hear ourselves think.

"Well?" she says.

We don't think we've ever seen quite so many bejeweled and bedazzling piercings on one person in all our lives. Clusters of ear and eyebrow rings. Nose rings. Nose chains. Tongue studs. The insouciant nubs of brassy nipple piercings jutting glintingly through the vaporous silk of her nearly see-through braless blouse. We don't care to further catalogue what we imagine south of the incredibly wide and bulky black belt barely holding her skirt to her curving flanks.

"Spill it, Lurch."

"Your face looks… vaguely angelic."

"I get that all the time. What's your problem?"

"We are not receiving the call we've been waiting for all our lives."

"Royal we?"

"Plural."

"But you're all alone here."

"So we've come to understand."

"Couldn't help noticing, is all. No muss, no fuss, no matter, your biz."

She smiles sideways at us and winks fetchingly.

;-)

"I mind my own."

"We're having trouble with our system," we manage.

"Trouble with our system," she muses, amused. Glancing disdainfully at our phone and tapping a black-lacquered nail to black-glossed lower lip, she seems mired in hopelessly depressing thought for a moment, when, suddenly, she places a warm hand on our chest, pushes us three steps backward to our sofa, and settles herself beside us, her stockinged thigh sparking static as it rubs against our khakied leg. She adjusts her hips with a deeply stirring pelvic wiggle. "Lumpy," she says. "Does this pull out into a bed?" She stretches an arm, rests it on the cushion behind our neck. Her fingernails graze our nape, sending chills goose-stepping willy nilly up our spine. We are beginning to perceive a pattern. We have perceived such a pattern before. The last time we perceived such a pattern, we ended up with a soon-to-be ex-spouse half our age.

"Yes," we say. "This is where we sleep."

"So this is where it all happens," Troubleshooter says.

"This is where what all happens?"

"Exactly. God *knows* what all happens here. The furtive, the shameful, the slick and icky." She sighs, touches hand to breast, eyes closed. "The things this sofa could tell *Penthouse Forum* if it could make up stories."

Her heat makes us sweat. She is young enough to be our eldest spouse's eldest daughter's daughter via teenaged indiscretion. We feel a moment's pang of compunction before shifting our weight from port to starboard buttock. "About our system," we hazard.

"Why, oh, why, oh, why," she cries, standing abruptly to face us. "Why do I always fall for pale, limp, and unflappable guys? Fun for an evening, sure, but despicable, weak, flabby, and farty in the long run. I just can't help myself sometimes, is all, but don't worry," she says, arms akimbo, glaring down her onyx nose stud at us. "This isn't one of those times. I'm a professional, and I'm on the clock, so don't get your dirty little hopes up." She pirouettes smoothly on the toe of a single spiked heel, then strides three long-legged steps to our computer. She flips it on, studies the screen, fingers flashing on the keyboard. "Your hardware's dreamy," she says, "loaded to the gigagills with magical possibility, a pubescent geekly hacker's wet dream of motherboarded, multihertzed megabytage."

"We built it ourselves."

"Well, it's built like the proverbial navel-stapled, spread-wide, in-the-pink centerfold slut you probably abuse yourself over nightly. I'm impressed. But your software," she says, rapidly tapping at the keyboard some more, daintily upturned nose sniffing dismissively, "your software's a goopy waste of disk space."

"We wrote it ourselves. Our problem," we endeavor to clarify, "is with our phone system."

"I'll say. No modem, for one thing, high speed or wait-for-it, and software that wouldn't let you do anything with a modem even if you had one. And not a single mouse in the house. A person could die of digital cramps with all this manual data entry." She turns back to the keyboard, types some more, studies the screen, pink tongue wetting her lower lip. "This is the scruffiest software I've ever seen," she says finally. "What*ever* do you *use* it for?

"Please don't disturb it," we say. "It belongs to our clients."

"Clients?"

"Certain key personnel in highly-placed government positions who pay us to crunch certain… entities."

"Explain."

"We are a freelance cruncher of entities by profession," we patiently explain. "Our clients, movers and shakers all, send us entity-laden disks in each day's mail. We insert said disks into our computer, extricate said entities from said disks, crunch said entit-ities, reorganize them in a critically-specified fashion, encapsulate them back onto said disks, and mail said said disks back to our clients, who pay us enough to support our various ex-spouses and children in a comfortable manner."

Troubleshooter's left hand toys with an unbuttoned button of her blouse. "You just said en*titty*tease," she giggles. "You dirty old man."

We blush. "Not precisely."

"Yes, you did. You certainly did. Is it hot in here, or is it just you?"

"*En*tities, we meant to say," we say.

She grins askance at us, winks mischievously.

; ->

"You naughty little splooger," she says. "What sorts of *entittytease*?"

"The generally abstract and abstruse ones," we say.

"E.g.?"

"Numbers, words, formulae, et al."

"I.e.?"

"Cyphers, cryptograms and -graphs, n-dimensional hyperbole."

"Could you be more, dot-dot-dot, specific?"

"Not in the nature of our line of work. Still, we can reassure you that most of what we crunch is pure and utter gibberish, both before and after we crunch it.

"Bottom line?"

"We enjoy a substantial mark-up. You name it, if it's gibberish, we crunch it."

"Signs, symbols, portents?"

"At present, all but portents. We wouldn't mind crunching portents, were a client to send a few our way. The future may well be in portents."

"You show a certain knack for the tautological."

"This is the reason our services remain in high demand. We have become the most tediously redundant and redundantly excessive cruncher of entities in our profession. When we crunch an entity, it stays crunched."

"Oh!" Troublshooter squeals, swiveling away from our computer and inserting index finger in pouting mouth. "I just broke a nail typing on your big, fat, stupid keyboard!"

"We're terribly sorry," we say.

"No, you're not."

"Yes, we really are."

"Then kiss it," she says.

"Excuse us?"

"If you're *really* terribly sorry, prove it. Kiss it and make it feel better."

We rise from sofa, bend to kiss the proffered finger's slightly chipped black lacquer.

"Kneel first."

"We beg your pardon?"

"You beg my pardon on your knees, slut-puppy."

We kneel, kiss her finger.

"Again," she says.

We kiss it again. She pushes her finger into our mouth, wiggles it. "Humiliating, isn't it," she says.

"Approxthimately," we mumble.

"Now suck."

"Mutht we?"

"Yes."

We suck.

"Yuck," she says. "Stop it."

We stop it.

"Get off your knees."

We stand.

"Go sit," she says.

We go to the sofa, look at her. She nods. We sit.

"Now, stay," she says. She narrows her bejeweled eyes at us, crosses left leg over right, slowly swivels back and forth, jiggling left foot so that tip of spiked heel traces the symbol for infinity mid-air. She draws in breath, closes her eyes. The shoe drops from her foot. She hums a softly off-key tune we do not recognize that gradually rises in both pitch and volume until it ends with a high-pitched shuddered gasp and a stiffening of her severely arched instep. Troubleshooter sighs, uncrosses legs, opens eyes. Her dilated pupils focus demurely. "And don't ever try anything like that again," she murmurs.

"What about our phone?" we say.

"Screw your phone."

We raise our eyebrows.

"No, just sit there. You're a sick one, you. You've gotten me so distracted, all I can think of is pinching those little pockets of tender flesh behind your earlobes until you squeak like a mouse."

"Sorry," we say. "We have little control over our effect on women."

"My, my," Troubleshooter observes. "Fairly full of ourselves, aren't we?"

"We who?" we say.

"We *whom*, you mean. We is you."

"We *are* you," we gently correct her.

"No, you're not," Troubleshooter says. "*I'm* me, and *you*, you're just full of yourself."

We make an effort to explain that, yes, we *are* fairly full of ourselves, and that we have been for as long as we can remember. We must confess that, like it or not, we've always found ourselves somehow… different, unique, unparalleled, *special*, even. And yet and still, we must further confess that, try as we might, so far we have never been able to obtain any empirical data to corroborate this finding, nor have we even the inklingest of the faintest idea of where to locate such data. Thus we wait for evidence to present itself. We wait for a certain call, a call we feel fairly certain will come one day, come what may, a call that will assure us beyond an umbra of a second guess that we are, indeed, in fact, in toto, our very own special selves.

"Are you on drugs?" Troubleshooter says.

"No."

"Have you considered them?"

"We have considered and tried many drugs in the past," we assure her, "both pharmaceutical and recreational. None served to bring us the call we have been waiting for. Thus we twelve-stepped our way away from all mind-altering substances, attending regular meetings where we drank black coffee, inhaled second-hand smoke, learned to meditate serenely and acceptingly on our station in life, and were known only by our first names, which we've since forgotten from disuse. Serene meditation and acceptance, we soon discovered, served no better in providing us with our call, and the coffee jangled our nerves, so we one-stepped our way away from our twelve-step program mid-step and have been waiting expectantly by our phone ever since. And yet and still," we say, boldly standing from the seat we were instructed to stay in, voice rising with our passionate rhetoric, "we grow fidgety, waiting patiently while our expectations remain ineluctably dashed. Thus our episode with the telephone. Thus Management's call to phoneman and phoneman's call to you. Will we never receive the call we have been waiting for all our lives? Please!" we plead, near tears at the power of our own rhetorical passion. "Can you, *will* you, help us?"

"Screaming heebie-jeebies," Troubleshooter muses. "Chill." Her face softens. "In a different time, a different place, under a different-colored moon, outfitted in hooded latex gear with leather-thonged accessories specifically suited to the job at hand, I could help you in ways you'd tremble to imagine…"

Troubleshooter throws us a sideways glance that masks her true emotions.

(:+0

"Oh, yes," she croons, "I could set your naughties on fire… but here, now, on the clock?"

"Please," we say. "We need a new system."

"System," she scoffs, mouth twisting. "Phoneman knows systems. *His* system has *never* been the solution. But I like the way you beg," she says, pulling a long, sharpened pencil from her décolletage, tapping its eraser reflectively against a gleaming tongue stud, and finally, grudgingly, making a notation in a black patent leather-bound dayplanner. "I'll have to rearrange my schedule to fit you in," she says, "but what the hell—show me your plastic, and I'll see what I can do."

"Phoneman said we should never show anyone our credit cards."

"That phoneman. Such a dweebly do-right. How'm I supposed to conjure without one?"

We show her a major credit card, which she takes from our hand (long fingernails tantalizing our moistened palm in an excruciatingly ticklish manner) and slides smoothly through a slot on her heretofore gratuitously oversized belt buckle. The buckle beeps.

"How much?" we ask uncertainly.

"As much as your credit can afford, ducks. I'll need some stuff from my sport-utility vehicle, but first I have to make a call."

"Did you just call us ducks?"

"No, you silly goose."

"Yes, you did. You called us ducks, we're certain."

"Don't contradict me, ducks. Let me make my call."

We let her make her call, overhear a high-pitched male voice fawning tinnily from the receiver, whining, "Yes, Mistress of my worthless loins!" and "Mother, may I, please?" to each of her softly-growled directives.

"You won't be needing this anymore," she says, pointing to our phone after hanging up. "The phoneman said something about a ball-ping hammer?"

"Ball-peen hammer."

"No good. I need a ball-ping hammer."

We go to our utility drawer, bring her our ball-peen hammer.

Her eyes dance. "This will do nicely."

"Perhaps we should explain our needs to you in more detail."

"Phoneman knew your needs," Troubleshooter says. "I know what you want, thanks and a tip o' the hat to Bobby Zimmerman, alt dot rock dot dylan… I have a word for you. Ask and it's yours."

We ask.

"Web," she whispers, and, to our disappointed silence, adds, "as in World Wide. I have another word. Ask."

We ask again.

"Hypertext transfer protocol," she mouths as if in prayer, "colon backslash backslash doubleyou doubleyou doubleyou dot—" soulfully—"wherever."

"That's a word?"

"In a word, yes. The most important word you'll need to learn. I have many other words for you, but first I'll need to disable your phone to install your modem."

She turns to our phone, hammer raised.

"But what of our call?"

She turns to us, snorting impatiently "How long have you had a phone?"

"All our lives."

"And how long have you been waiting for this so-called call?"

"Ibid."

"Your problem is obvious. The so-called call you've been waiting for is actually a message, and what better way to receive a message than by access to the Internet, an anarchic, chaotic plethora of messages being sent and received ceaselessly even as we speak, just on the other side of your phone jack there. You need to tap into these messages. You don't want a phone, you want a modem, high speed, and as soon as I get my stuff from my sports-utility vehicle, I plan to hook you up to the fastest system your credit can buy."

"Couldn't we simply leave the phone in place?"

"Nope."

"Why not?"

"I don't like the looks of it."

"Couldn't we simply hide it in a drawer?"

Troubleshooter licks her pouting lips. "What fun would that be?"

She delicately caresses the ball-peen's shaft, tip of tongue poking from pursed lips.

<:-|-

Then, with studious concentration and a sure-handed swing, she goes right to work.

"What's cooking?" Troubleshooter says several hours later. "I'm starving."

"Our dinner," we say. "Would you care for some?"

She rises from our work station, stretches tawny muscles beneath tight white satin and lace, peers over our shoulder at dinner steaming in the microwave. "What is it?" she says.

"Our regular calorically monitored evening meal," we say. "We'll set you a place at our galley kitchen countertop."

She sniffs dubiously. "Is it any good?"

"It has the capacity for being neither pleasing nor especially displeasing."

"No thanks," she decides. "Anyway, I'm done. Welcome to the twenty-first century. Come here."

The microwave beeps.

"I said *come!*"

We come.

"Phoneman was right about one thing, you know. You *do* need to get out more. But that doesn't mean leaving home. I set you up with the finest starter kit your credit could buy," she says, "and your credit can buy the finest there is. I've opened a web site for you, complete with blog…"

She points the cursor at a desktop icon showing a bony, naked man with his head stuck entirely up his fundament, and a coding banner appears:

```
<a href="http://www.webeus.net/call.html">
```

"A place of your own where cybercitizens can stop by, learn something concerning your hot new wants and needs, and IM you. No more waiting for that certain special call. Now you can actively *solicit* it. BTW, I'll need a photo of you to scan onto your page ASAP. Take off all your clothes and get your digital camera."

"We don't have one."

"Pity. Keep your clothes on for now, then. I'm on the clock, after all… I also took the liberty of subscribing you to several interesting newsgroups:

```
<alt.sex.whimper-suk>
<alt.fetish.foot-n-mouth>
<alt.bondage.anal-jam>
<alt.othersex.etc-et-al>
```

which point you to teeming, writhing mass chat rooms and virtual play, all handily referenced on your Favorites drop-down. You can add new sites, groups, and rooms whenever the desire, ahem, arises."

"We're not certain—"

"*Exactly!*" she interrupts, and we prudently refrain from commenting on her rudeness. "That's your problem. You're uncertain. But the real problem is you'll *never* be certain. You need to get comfortable with uncertainty. That's where *this* system comes in. Cyberspace is fraught with uncertainty. You can never be certain that the surgically endowed, whip-stroking blonde bunker buster you've been playing virtual footsie with in a darkened corner of a certain fetish lounge I've visited (and linked to your Bookmark, don't mention it) isn't IRL (that's *in real life*, ducks) a certain seemingly dull and superannuated recluse with a latent yet budding yen for strap-on homoerotic foreplay *avec* rubber ball-gag who claims he crunches entities for a living, if you catch my drift. What *is* reality, ducks?" she says, cupping a hand at the crotch of her dress and squeezing authoritatively.

"You called us a duck again."

"Ducks. Plural. Get over it."

"But will we still be able to crunch our entities?" we ask, more uncertain now than ever we've felt in all our lives.

"Better than ever. That's the beauty. I also took the liberty of opening your Accounts Receivable file (impressive!), locating your clients, tracing their e-mail addresses, and memoing off new transfer protocol for sending and receiving pre-crunched and crunched entities in easily up- and downloaded ziplocked files. Directory and instructions are loaded right onto your old program. Just click on *Help*. No more waiting for your work to arrive in the daily snail-mail. Instant access and transmission. No more waiting for that one mythical special call. Multi-media messages at the touch of a mouse."

"And all this will solve our problem?"

"And more."

"Your guarantee?"

"Oh," she sighs, hand fluttering at breast, "in another place, late at night, software softly humming, hard drive winking crimson, one hand stroking your mouse, the other yearning to grope experimentally south of your keyboard, elbows tethered (not *too* constrictively) together near the small of your back, trust me, I could give a guarantee that would tickle the soft and sagging armpits of your very soul." She takes a deep breath, slowly releases it. "But here and now is neither the place nor time. I still have other calls to make." She packs up her equipment and approaches us, standing unbearably close.

"Click me sometime," she says, smiling devilishly.

};^-)

"I'm on your desktop. And don't look so forlorn, ducks. Once you're up and running and all those messages from all sorts of people you never even knew existed come zipping in, you'll forget you were ever waiting for one measly call."

She hooks a finger in our waistband, pulls us even closer. Her lips pucker an air-kiss near our ear, hot breath crackling with voltage. "Ciao," she whispers, and with that, she breezes out the door, a sense of hot lace trailing in her wake.

We return to our meal, which has grown cold. We discover that the temperature of our meal in no way adds to nor diminishes from its generally pleasant or unpleasant qualities.

We chow.

net-lude

We click our cursor on Troubleshooter's Uniform Resource Locator on our desktop, represented by an icon of Botticelli's "Venus" masturbating with a whip handle. Explorer begins exploring:

```
<http://www.lix&sux.com/ambidom.chix.w/surprises.html>
```

We go to our galley kitchen and make ourselves a cup of soothing caffeine-free tea while our computer patiently pulls up streaming megadoses of text, audio, video, steamingly graphic real-time graphics and countless links leading to image after image of sexually stunning decadence.

We are no longer impressed by such symbolic gestures.

Our DNA no longer feels called upon to replicate itself.

When we return, Troubleshooter's now-familiar black-hooded visage, black-corseted bosom, black-leather-booted calves, and black-latex crotchless-pantied crotch await us:

COME, SLAVE!
THE MIZTERESS COMMANDS YOU!

We click and are offered a menu. We click again and are routed through several more menus until we are deposited at the ornately gargoyled doorway of Troubleshooter's own personal chat chamber.

Once again, for perhaps the hundredth time in only a few weeks, we log in (or *on*, we are none too certain which) and request entrance. We observe the symbolically debasing obeisance of prostrating ourselves and applying IRL tongue to the screen's virtual sole of the Mizteress's (we have been assured by a grainy depiction) "stinking boot whose spiked heel has just this minute been withdrawn from the diarrhetic derriere of a previous supplicant!" and are instantly whisked in.

The Mizteress (in real-time streaming video) is idly whipping a slight and long-haired young man with the look of a poet about his bruised lips. He winces, naked and bound spread-eagled to a brass bed, bottom up, as the Mizteress turns from him to type on her keyboard.

A sidebar scrolls as she types a string of obscenities, ending with "More, slaves?"

As has become our habit, we announce our presence by virtually "knocking" on our asterisk button, (a method of introduction we take no small amount of satisfaction in having recently invented ourselves), thus:

```
US:              ***********************************???
```

As has become characteristic of the other denizens of this chat room, explained perhaps, if not mitigated, by their collective furtive desires reaching coincidentally and simultaneously a certain satiated crescendo at our arrival (once again), the chamber swiftly empties.

```
Diaperboy:      Fuckhead alert!
4gimme:         Adios, I'm outa here.
NAUGHTY-2-U:    Just when it was starting to HURT
wuss:           gotta run beat me later
WHIP&WIPE:      We have met the enemy & he is
US:             ****************************???!!??
                We hope we haven't interrupted at
                an inopportune moment.
SwAlLoW HoLe:   Got a mouse in his pocket?
-rich:          I'm all soft again--------groan.
```

                @yr.cervx: not ur fault dickless. ull
                                 getitup again........
                Mztrs: What's going on, slaves?
                ALL (but 1):   Buttbrain alert. Bolting 4 now.
                                 Service you tomorrow.

Which importune message is followed by a fortuitous mass exit that leaves us quite alone with Troubleshooter, not counting the spread-eagled poet, who by the entreating look on his face wishes the "Emptress of [his] girlish loins" were never interrupted by ours truly. "Er, excuse us," we type. "This sort of thing seems to happen all the time."

                Mztrs: Not u again.
                US: Yes. It is we. Us. We are delighted
                                 to find you in. Er. On. Line. Sorry.
                Mztrs: U will pay slave. I have ur credit
                                 card number and plan on conjuring
                                 bigtime. Where have all the other
                                 supplicants gone? I wasnt finished
                                 toying w/ them.
                US: We suppose they must have gone where
                                 they generally go when we log on.
                                 Um. Log in? As a rule, they log out
                                 or off whenever we begin to say or
                                 rather type somrthinf.
                Mztrs: When did u type somrthinf?
                US: Just a moment ago. But "Something,"
                                 we meant to say. Er. Type. Sorry. Our
                                 fingers get nervous in unsettling
                                 situations such as those inspired by
                                 your chamber.

The long-haired poet writhes in his shackles, apparently and soundlessly begging for further attention. Troubleshooter ignores him, choosing instead to stare at her webcam (and thus us) with increasingly impatient frustration.

                Mztrs: ENOUGH!!! Uv been my best customer
                                 these past few weeks but ur killing
                                 my bizness. What the fuck do u want

this time???? Apparently none of
this!

Troubleshooter idly backhands her whip across the poet's bare
buttocks. He shivers in ecstasy.

US: Oh, please, Troubleshooter, please, we want

Mztrs: DO NOT CALL ME BY THAT NAME HERE!

US: our phone back. We want our old lives back. We do not care for the web with all its sticky netiquette. We feel lost and hopeless. We've worked on our homepage for weeks and weeks, even letting our clients' entities pile up in our inbox uncrunched, and still we receive no messages, let alone the message you said would come in place of the call we have been waiting all our lives for—for which we have been waiting, etc., but of course you understand.

Mztrs: Um. Understand what exactly?

US: That we have calculated our page's "hits" in the thousands since first we went online, and yet all those hits result in misses when we receive no messages in return. Chatrooms empty at our entrance; newsgroups drop from the directory shortly after we join a thread. For example, "We neither agree and/nor disagree with all that's been posted re: ennui," we recently posted to the alt.angst. existential group, "although we do experience some difficulty caring which needle's eye this particular thread's amateurish philosophy squints its way through, when more crucial to us is the fact that we continue to fail to receive the one specifically scrumptious call we

have been waiting/delete/for which
we have been waiting all our lives,
complimentary closure," and no
sooner had we pressed enter than we
discovered that the subscription base
of said angst newsgroup had fallen
from 13,666 to 1, the latter being
us, we presumed, before unsubscribing
ourselves ourselves. Please,
Troubleshooter. Er. Mizteress.
Please, help us!

Mztrs: ...

US: Are you there? Please don't tell us
you've logged off or out too!

We look up from our keyboard. On our screen, Troubleshooter is nowhere in sight. Neither is her keyboard, which usually rests on an ornate table bestrewn with vibrators, whips, handcuffs, cattle prods, and various lubricants, betwixt wrought-iron headboard (now on camera) and medieval rack (now off). The tortured poet hangs melancholic from his trusses, staring accusingly at us.

A message suddenly appears:

Mztrs: hmmm...

US: Yes? Troubleshooter?

Mztrs: I TOLD U DONT FUCKING CALL ME THAT
HERE!!!

US: YES, MIZTERESS, WE HEAR AND OBEY!

Mztrs: AND TAKE OFF YOUR FUCKING CAP LOCK!!!

US: Yes, Mizteress.

Mztrs: Thats better. Now beg me for my help.

US: We beg you.

Mztrs: Beg better.

US: We truly, really, actually,
verifiably, and beseechingly beg you.
Um. Where are you?

Mztrs: In the bathroom. Thanx to a wireless
keyboard. Dont u wish u were here
with me changing my bloody tampon?

US: ...

Mztrs: Ur no fun. Thats ur problem. I was
afraid of this. Ur just not good
net material. I tried my best & as
the warranty on all of my services
states I cant be held responsible for
customer dissatisfaction caused by
system misapplication. I cant help
u...but I know of someone who might.

US: Who?

Mztrs: His name is Bob aka Crazy Bob but
word is never call him that to his
face. I can try to contact him. It
wont be eady. Hes the Dalai Lama of
geeks. Rumor is he programmed for
MicroMac until he wrote a program so
dangerously advanced and virtually
free that they terminated his
contract. Bob went indie. Turned
from software to hardware which hes
supposed to be some kind of prodigy
at. IF & thats a big IF I get in
touch with him thru a Byzantine super
secret email routing system that
looks like an MC Escher print & IF
hes interested ull hear from him. If
not ur on ur own.

US: We see. We think. BTW, "...at which
he's supposed to be some kind of
prodigy," we think you meant to
say or rather type, not to mention
"easy" instead of "eady" back there
somewhere. And apparently your
apostrophe key is out of commission
again.

Our tortured poet has fallen to sleep. A soft smile plays around his
drooling lips. He seems extremely comfortable, despite the shackles
biting into his wrists and ankles. If only we could sleep so soundly.

Mztrs: I could have loved u u know. On a
different baud speed using a wholly
alien dialect of hypertext mark-

                    up language. Ur babysoft orifices
                    brightly pierced. Ur crimson labials
                    stretched tight by a red rubber
                    ball-gag. The puckered * of ur rosy
                    fundament smiling shyly up at me. But
                    instead u insist on disappointing me.
US: We're uncertain quite how we've
                    disappointed you, but we apologize
                    all the same.
Mztrs: Thats ur problem. Always uncertain.
                    Some people wait lifetimes to get a
                    message like mine. A message u insist
                    on being uncertain of.

And with that she logs off, breaking our connection.

Hopes left dangling like Troubleshooter's final preposition, we pull the plug on our computer, crashing our system in our haste to log our way off, out, and away from her forever.

cloister-rom

Our days go by. Our shattered phone remains ringless, our computer bipless. Our profession ceases to satisfy us. "We feel biserable," we enable our e-mail program to respond to any and all concerned clients. "We will dot be crudjig eddidies today. We bust be comig dowd wid a code."

Our microwave beeps, day after day, but all that we eat from it tastes of ashes and dust. We begin to perceive a pattern, and, we realize, have probably been perceiving such a pattern all along. Our meals neither please nor displease, nor do they fill the emptiness inside us. Ashes, ashes, we think-sing to ourselves between mouthfuls, we all fall down. All, we have begun to realize, all is for nothing.

Still, we wait. We sit on our made-up sofabed, head inclined, eyes open, staring at our ceiling. We begin to see a pattern in the patternless popcorn plaster suspended above. The pattern neither pleases nor displeases us. We wait. We are used to waiting. We have been waiting all our lives now, waiting for a call that will tell us something grand and true and beautiful and special and indubitably delicious about ourselves, a call that will not only presently change our lives at present but will retroactively change our past lives as well, will make our future lives as clean and sweet and new and improved as puddled honey 'neath a thriving hive of slap-sappy bee-bees.

Happy bees, we think we mean to say. We no longer know what we think we mean to say.

With phone decommissioned now and computer on hold, we no longer have access to any calls. Thus we decide to wait for a time before returning to waiting for our call. We wait. We stare at our ceiling. We rise periodically to prepare and eat a regularly scheduled, calorically monitored meal. We stare at our ceiling some more.

Popcorn. Patterns. We wait to wait.

We could wait like this for quite some indeterminate length of time, we think.

•

Our intercom buzzes. We rise.

"Who is it?" we ask.

"Bob."

"Bob whom?"

"That'd be 'Bob who?'" a thinly cracking voice answers. "Don't be such an anal-retentive grammar hound. Some chick eemed me, said you had a problem."

"Troubleshooter, you mean?"

"I'm basically clueless. Feminine syntax, imperative sentences like a Gestapo officer's wet dream."

"That would be she."

"Glad we're clear. Buzz me up, Scotty."

"Our name isn't Scotty."

"I know that, Bob."

"Our name isn't Bob, either."

"I know that too, Bob. But calling everybody Bob—a name, coincidentally, that I can remember like my own—happens to save me a lot of brain cells. And brain cells are knowledge, Bob, and knowledge is energy, and energy never dies. Ipso facto, I'm dying down here when I could be up there solving your fucking problem. Excuse my fucking French, Bob. Buzz me up ASAP."

"We're no longer interested in your services," we say. "We've solved our own problem."

"Have we now. I doubt it. But more important, I happen to have a little problem of my own. I rode my bicycle crosstown to get here, and the way I see it, you owe me for a service call, even if you don't want the service anymore. Plus of which I gotta take a wicked pee. Let me up to use your bathroom."

"We prefer not to."

"I'm gonna pee on your stoop, motherfucker, excuse my inner-city-ese. I'm busting the old tinkle dance down here. No charge on that service call if you just let me up. Please?"

"There's a convenience store two blocks east."

"I'll never make it. Plus they look at you funny unless you buy something. Even when you buy something, they still look at you funny. What is it with these funny looking convenience store people? Buzz me up, Bob, I'm starting to dribble."

"We're sorry," we say. "We can't."

"Sure you can. Just press the button. Pretty please?"

"Again," we say, "sorry."

"You ever hear of Kitty Genovese, Bob? Trust me. You don't want a tragedy occurring on your doorstep that'll make you a case study in callous disregard for a fellow human being's bursting bladder. Let me in!"

We release the intercom button, return to our sofa, sit. The intercom buzzes several more times then falls silent. We sigh, relieved, and continue our waiting.

There is a sharp, staccato knock at our apartment door. A louder knock, followed by what we surmise to be several kicks. We rise and unlatch all but the chain lock, peer through the open crack.

It is a boy.

Dressed in untucked baggy t-shirt and low-riding jeans, he shuffles a pigeon-toed jig on the tiptoes of his sneakered feet, face a twisted mask of agony. "Lemme in lemme in lemme in!" he cries pitifully.

We let him in.

"Bathroom bathroom bathroom!" he gasps, spinning in wild, panicky circles in the center of our efficiency. He quickly locates the only other door in the apartment and slams through it. Our toilet lid, which we always keep down, crashes against the porcelain tank, and we hear the gushing impact of water on water for quite some time until it slowly dribbles to a tinkling conclusion.

"Woof," he says, exiting the bathroom without washing his hands. "I think I did some renal damage, holding it that long." He swipes a sweaty strand of ebony hair from his forehead. It joins a sleek sprawl of shoulder-length locks before flopping back down over his eyes. He pauses mid-room to eye us up and down.

"You OK?" he says.

"We've felt better."

"I mean for me to be in the same room with. You look like a serial killer in search of a do-it-yourself project. I'm guessing you're mostly self-destructive, but reassure me. Promise me you won't hurt me."

"We won't hurt you," we promise.

"Not even my feelings. Promise."

"We promise we will do our best to avoid hurting you or your feelings," we say.

"Hope your best is good enough." He holds out an unwashed hand to shake. "I'm Bob," he says.

We put our hands behind our back, smile, shake our head apologetically, and Bob smoothly continues the motion of his outstretched hand upward to comb through his tangled tresses.

"We hab a code," we offer. "How did you gain entrance through the security door downstairs?"

"So easy I wonder why you even ask." Bob glances around our efficiency, sniffs. "What's that smell?" he says.

"Our dinner."

"Phew. I'd open a window."

"Our apartment has none."

He frowns. "Isn't that against the Building Cold?"

"Pardon us?"

Bob rolls his eyes. "I never explain my clever repartees, Bob. Wow," he says, moving to our work station, "check out the Smithsonian exhibit."

"Troubleshooter said our hardware was impressive."

"She needs to get out more. Actually, it's state of the art for a year ago. But I don't care if it's five minutes ago, all computers are museum pieces a week after you buy 'em. You can thank MicroMac and their Detroit assembly line tactics for that. Always hold off on the better product till next season. That's why I'll never buy a computer."

"But we understood that you were supposed to be a computer wizard."

"I am. I don't buy 'em, though. I build 'em." He sits in our swivel chair, switches on our computer. "I could fix this for you easy," he says.

We notice a silk-screened phrase emblazoned blackly across the back of his t-shirt: I'D RATHER BE THINKING, with the letters KIN crossed out and the resultant THING circled and slashed through in what appears to be red magic marker.

"There's nothing wrong with our computer," we inform him.

"That's what they all say. Hang on a sec."

We hang on several secs while Bob works his way into our registry—a place even we fear to visit—and begins a flurry of animated typing, pausing now and then to glance at the screen. The computer buzzes and whirs.

"There," Bob says after a time. "Nothing major, just a little reorganization of most of the crap you got on here, but I've pretty much doubled your RAM. Problem solved, Bob. I'm starved. How about ordering us a pizza?"

"Our problem was not with our computer," we say.

"Oh. Well, order us a pizza anyway."

"We must decline. Our diet dictates against all foods with perceptible flavor. However, we thank you all the same for your time and trouble in doubling our random access memory. How much do we owe you?"

"Order me a pizza and we'll call it even. Triple cheese, nothing else. Which is closer, Pizza Hut or Dominoes?"

"We have no idea."

"OK. Try this. Which is greasier, Pizza Hut or Dominoes?"

"Once again, we haven't the faintest."

"Take a wild one."

"Dominoes?"

"BAAAMP!" Bob says. "Pizza Hut is greasier. But Dominoes is slimier. It's the sauce. They use slimy tomatoes, I'm guessing. Order Pizza Hut. You can dab off most of the grease with a paper towel."

"We're sorry to report that we have no phone."

"What's this?" Bob says, poking through the shattered relic still in pieces on our countertop.

"As you can see, it is no longer in working order."

"The fuck you say," Bob says, "excuse my telecom-ese." He picks up several phoneshards, squints as if inspecting a precious archeological discovery. "Ball-peen hammer? I'm guessing, but it's an educated guess."

"Ball-ping hammer," we say, "but that's amazing."

He shrugs. "Lemme have a screwdriver, pliers, roll of duct tape, and some wire."

We fetch tools and tape. "We appear to be wireless at present," we say.

"Hmmm," he hums, already working with screwdriver. "No wire at all?"

"We have several wire coat hangers."

"No good, Mommy Dearest. How about a can of Coke and some sharp scissors you don't mind me dulling?"

"Will a Diet Sprite do?"

Bob shudders. "In a pinch."

Bob drains the Diet Sprite in several frenzied gulps, belches proudly, begins to snip long, curling, delicate strips from the recyclable aluminum container. "This'll take a minute," he says, "if you got something better to do than stare at me."

We nod, return to our sofa, recline our head back, continue perusing our ceiling.

Oh! The patterns!

"Done," Bob announces after a time. He hands us our taped-together phone. "You make the call, Bob. I already programmed Pizza Hut's number. Just hit memory dial. A large, triple-cheese pan pizza, easy on the grease."

"Why don't you call?" we say.

"I don't do calls," Bob says. "People are funny on the phone. Hurry it up. I gotta get back to my sitter soon. Me and her have an arrangement. My parents pay her to watch me, and I pay her to let me go on service calls."

"That would be 'She and I have an arrangement,' Bob."

"Ha!" Bob cries triumphantly. "I *knew* I could make you say 'I'! You're pretty weirdly wired, Bob, I hope you know, but it takes all kinds. I can't believe they still make me have a sitter. It's mortifying. I'm like, 'Hey, I'm not a baby anymore. I'm practically thirteen!' And they go, 'We know that, son, but we feel you need to mature a bit more.' I'm, 'Ma*too*er! I gotcher ma*too*rity for ya right *here*. Your darling son's Johnson grew a whole inch last year, and you're saying I ain't ma*too*er?' My dad, he's so mature I hear him making these Curly on the Three Stooges *nyuk-nyuk-nyuk* sounds late at night from their bedroom when they think I'm asleep. Could be worse, I guess. Could be those Shemp *eeebeedeebee* sounds."

Bob sighs, rolls his eyes, drums his knuckles on our galley kitchen countertop. "Puberty's hell."

He appears to be the sort of animated, energetic, carefree, fun-loving boy we might have fathered our very own selves with one of our ex-spouses years ago when we were more able in that arena, a son to whom we might even now be pitching baseballs, tossing footballs, teaching the finer arts of entity crunching, were our genes not of the more or less non-athletic and taciturn variety and were we not too busy waiting to wait for our call.

"Plus my mom's like this Amish drill instructor," Bob goes on. "'Your father and I feel that you need to take on more responsibility around the house as far as picking up after yourself and taking care of your things,' she tells me this morning before she goes to work. I'm like, 'Du-*uh*, Mom,' like as if every clock, DVR, and DVD player in the house wouldn't be flashing midnight for all eternity if it wasn't for yours truly. I'm like, 'Mom, it's *easy, look*, the TiVo comes with an instruction manual and *everything*, and she's like, 'Oh, I don't have the time to read those things.'"

Bob scratches his nose. Then he picks it. He looks at what he's picked. We avert our eyes queasily, and when we look at him again, whatever it is he's picked has disappeared. We hate to think where.

"I'm telling you, Bob, you think *you* got problems, you should try living at *my* house. Plus I'm supposed to be a genius and everything, which doesn't make things any easier. My dad supposedly has an IQ of like 160, but you wouldn't know it to listen to him. He starts every lecture with, 'If you're so smart…' My mom's IQ's higher than his, and she's like, 'Listen to your father, honey.' I'm smarter than the both of them squared, and I got no IQ. I refused to take the test."

"Why?"

"It was stupid. I wrote my own test. All these experts are still studying it. Like *they'll* pass it. Yeah, right. I'm telling you, Bob, much as I hated it, I'd rather be programming for MicroMac again than sit through one more dinner conversation with my parents. They're like essentially a clue short of Professor Plum in the Library with an Uzi, if you know what I mean. Please, Bob, I'm starving to death. Make the call, will you, huh, puh-*lease?*"

We make the call.

"Interesting life you're leading here," Bob says while we wait for delivery. "What do you do for entertainment?"

"Up until recently," we say, "we've spent no small amount of time crunching our entities."

"Uh-huh, uh-huh, uh-huh," Bob says, settling himself at our work station and flipping on our computer again. His legs dangle precociously short of the floor in our swivel chair.

"But we spend most of our time now staring at our ceiling."

"Uh-huh, I hear you, uh-huh. No TV, I notice."

"Little interest. Counterproductive."

"Sure, if you watch it in real time. Me, I record fifteen to twenty hours of programming per day—and haven't you ever wondered why they call it 'programming'?—but I watch it all on fast forward in like twenty or thirty minutes. I fixed my DVD player so it gives me audio on fast forward. My mom makes me wear headphones. She says it sounds like Alvin and the Chipmunks on acid. She used to be a hippie, and she freaks easy. Burned a lot of synapses behind her."

"You are a curious young man, Bob," we offer. "How can a boy your age know so much?"

Bob shrugs. He has entered, we see now, our Favorites drop-down menu and is idly bringing up various flashing screens of questionable imagery. "Dudes at ISB are still arguing, but the best-guess consensus right now is I use nineteen percent more of my brain than the average genius. I'm shooting for twenty."

"ISB?"

"Institute for the Study of Bob," he says. "That's me. National Science Foundation's funding the thing. They wanted to give me a grant to join the team studying myself, but my parents said no. They think I'm way too self-absorbed anyway. Whoa!" Bob gasps, stopping at the Mysterious Mizteress's page. "This stuff is *hot*." He frowns. "I'm not gonna stumble on any kiddy porn or anything here, am I, Bob?"

"How did you log in or on without our password?" we say.

"Gimme a break. It's too easy." Bob studies the Mizteress's latexed visage. "Because if there's any, like, kiddy porn stuff here, I'm out the door right now. I don't mind your adult porn between consenting deviates and all, but if my parents ever caught me getting involved with any pedophile links or chatlines, they'd pull the plug on my system and ground me for a year. Course I got an alternate back-up power source they don't know about, but still, that baby-love stuff is disgusting and creepy, IMO."

"No pedophilia," we say, "and no real consenting adult porn… except"—guiltily—"the site at which you've just arrived. Troubleshooter's domain, which link she installed herself on our desktop and we felt duty-bound to visit."

"This is the Troubleshooter?" Bob says. Bob scrunches forward in his seat, draws too deep a breath. "The one who eemed me about you?"

"Please," we say. "Go no further."

Bob gazes at her, eyebrows raising.

"Mom!" he says. Then, "Just kidding. Wonder if she does any babysitting." He glances at us, blushes. "I got this hormonal thing kicking in, in case you didn't notice. Voice cracking, zits popping, hair boldly growing where no hair grew before, nocturnal visits to the large economy-size Kleenex box. Old news to you, I'm sure."

"We vaguely recall," we offer.

"What the—" Bob bends closer to the screen. "Is that a dick, Bob?"

"Excuse us?"

"Picture's super grainy, but I swear this chick's got a little wood poking through those crotchlesses."

"Impossible," we say. "We met her. She sat on our sofa with us."

"Eeeyew," Bob says. "*Chacun a son gout,* excuse my French. Could be some kind of strap-on, I guess, but I wouldn't bet against the she-male theory. I'd join her group grope and ask, but I don't do virtual. First off, everybody lies like crazy. Second thing, virtual's way overrated. Takes too much imagination. I like my entertainment effort free. Leaves the brain cells open for more important business, like solving your problem. And speaking of your problem, Bob," he says, clicking off the image, "I look on your Net-works and despair." Bob swivels back and forth in our swivel chair, sneakered feet swinging. "You lied to me, Bob," he says gently. "You still haven't received your call."

"How do you know about our call?"

"Elementary, my dear Bobson. Just follow the smoke signals and you find the fire, even if the fire isn't burning anymore. I can retrieve and print off every word you've ever keystroked on this baby. Nothing's ever *really* erased, Bob. Nothing's deleted. There's a world of signals out there, man, and none of them ever die. You don't believe me, ask the Pentagon. Course, they'd lie, but what do you think they invented this system for? So a bunch of one-handed typists could stay up late at night taking turns rubbing their eyes and yanking their crankies?"

"We have no idea."

"You said it. So fill me in, Bob. I can't work without details. What kind of call are we waiting for, and who's this call supposed to be coming from? I need info. Gimme."

We try our best to explain as rationally as we can the nature of the call we have been waiting for all our lives, but we find ourselves growing increasingly frustrated with our inability to express our feelings precisely.

"Indescribably delicious," Bob muses after we've trailed off to a less than satisfying conclusion. "Special assurance of extra special status in the universal scheme of things. Gee, Bob, and they call *me* crazy?"

Recalling Troubleshooter's warning, we avert our eyes noncommittally.

"You surprise me, Bob," Bob says. "I like that. I mean, sure, you're like several noids short of human, but I can sorta kinda relate. I mean, for instance, I don't like talking on the phone much, so I never answer it when it rings. That's what Mom, Dad, and the answering machine're for, right? But this one time our machine got zapped by lightning, outa order, at the bottom of my Things-to-Fix list, and Mumsy's at work and Pa's playing tennis with a client and my Advanced Quantum Philosophy tutor from the university's running late as usual (home-schooling, doncha know) and the babysitter bailed for a minute to buy an emergency box of feminine protection (blush) and I'm in the middle of this rare moment home alone, when the phone rings.

"Well, Bob, let me tell you, I'm ninety-nine-point-nine-nine-nine percent positive the phone's not for me—anybody I do business with uses e-mail—but all of a sudden my ears prick up and I feel this like crackhead jonesing urge to answer that phone, even though I don't want to, you know? No, it's more like this *Call of the Wild* com*pul*sion. It's like this Pavlovian programmed stimulus-response hierarchical salivating imperative, Bob. I'm getting the shakes just remembering it. Vision tunneling, blood pressure soaring. If I had fur on my neck it'd be standing on end, dude. I feel like this dog we used to have before he died in a tragic accident I don't like to talk about. Lab retriever, supposed to love the water, OK? But you couldn't get him in the pool, even in the dog days of summer, 'cause when he was just a pup, before we got him, before he was weaned even, he accidentally fell in his mother's owner's swimming pool. Nobody human around to help him, mother too preoccupied with a half-dozen pups sucking her teats (I like that word) to notice the runt strayed off, the runt himself too small to climb out on his own, and so he just puppy-paddled himself to exhaustion before the owner discovered him and fished him out half-dead a couple hours later. Trauma induced a literal case of hydrophobia by the time we bought him. He'd drink the water, but you couldn't lead him anywhere near a pool. If you tried, even with a choke chain, he'd just hit the deck, dig in his claws, splay himself out in this pitiful impression of the results of that frog-tossed-to-the-sidewalk-from-a-third-story-biology-lab experiment: wouldn't budge.

"So one hot summer Sunday afternoon I figure I'm gonna cure him of this phobia. My dad's grilling steaks on the patio barbie. Dog's slavering around waiting for a chop to drop. I'm in the pool, calling to him, over and over, 'Here, Bob! Come inna pool, Bob! Go for a 'lil swim, Bob!' And he's like 'Duh, no thanks, Bob!' My dad laughs and says, 'Give it a rest, son, you'll never get him in there,' and he goes in the house for another beer. That's when I make my move. I grab the tongs, pick a sizzly steak off the fire, hold it up so the juice is dripping right onto the dog's tongue while he jumps in the air trying to grab it, and then I walk into the shallow end of the pool, hold the steak out for him to see. Tempting, huh?

"Dog just stares at me, head tilted in that clueless doggy way they have. 'Here, Bob,' I tell him. 'Come in and get your steak, Bob.' Well, Bob, the realization of what's really going on finally hits that dog, and I gotta tell you, I got a whole new respect for the term Approach-Avoidance Syndrome that afternoon. I mean, the dog just stood there on the edge of the pool, tail curved straight up at attention, staring at me and my steak, like he was paralyzed or something, his little doggy pea-brain just feeding this looped message round and round the inside of his pointy little skull—steak *good*, water *bad*—over and over for what had to be the longest inert waking moment of his simple doggy life, over and over, thesis and antithesis, with no synthesis in sight, 'Here, Bob, c'mon, Bob,' frozen in place like a bronzed doggy statue. He didn't even whine or drool. Just stared at that steak I was holding just above the water. But I swear I could sense him like subatomically *vibrating* the whole time, like the little quarks and leptons inside the nuclei of his atoms were spinning faster and faster and still getting nowhere. But so I watched him in frozen motion like that, me still holding the beef, 'Here, Bob,' through the whole two-minute ordeal, thinking if this went on I'd maybe be the first person in the history of the world to like spontaneously combust a dog, until my dad came back out and told me to quit tormenting the poor mutt."

Bob shakes his head sorrowfully.

"That's kinda sorta what I felt like listening to that phone ring, is why I mentioned it in the first place. Well, not *exactly*, I guess. I wasn't about to catch on fire or anything, but ninety-nine-point-etcetera percent of me is saying, 'Fuck it, let it ring.' But it's one of those persistent calls where they let it ring past five rings, past *ten* rings, working our way towards *twenty fucking rings*, Bob. And the whole time it's ringing, this little point-zero-zero-zero-one percent of me is sweating it, saying '*Answer*, you moron, it could be im*por*tant, for fucksake!'"

Bob stands panting and trembling, fists clenched, knuckles white, face bloodless. He closes his eyes, takes several deep breaths to calm himself. "So I guess I'm saying I can relate, Bob," he says, finally.

"We see," we say uncertainly. "To what?"

"To you and your call thing, Bob. What else? I mean, we're programmed to think every call could be somehow important. Why else pick up the phone? So you just took your programming a metalogical step further, OK? If all these calls you're getting are unimportant, but you're still picking up the phone, then ipso facto, Q.E.D., there *must* be a *really* important call out there somewhere waiting for you to answer it. You'd be like my dog if he finally jumped in, only I deep-sixed the steak where he couldn't find it. He'd be paddling all over the pool going, 'Where's the steak, Bob? I *know* it's here *some*where!' Isn't that kinda how you feel, Bob, like a waterlogged hydrophobic dog swimming around the pool of life looking for something good to eat?"

"Well," we say as politely as we are able, "not precisely."

"Well," Bob says sardonically, "just fuck me, then, excuse my Greek. Another metaphor for life down the proverbial drain." Bob crosses his eyes, slaps his bang-strewn forehead. "What a waste of brain cells. What I'm saying, I guess, is this compulsion to pick up the phone when it rings would make a lot more sense if one day you picked it up and the clouds above parted and, like, this chorus of angels line-danced their way across the sky, singing, 'Holy! Holy! Holy! Please remain on the line for a very special message just for you!'"

"We can't argue with that kind of reasoning, Bob," we say. "But did you ever answer the phone?"

"Yeah. After about the zillionth ring. Fucking phone solicitor. Computer-generated voice, no less."

We nod knowingly. "And what of your dog?" we ask, voice funereally low. "You mentioned a tragic accident, we recall?"

"Defunct," Bob says. "Choked on the steak I gave him when I got out of the pool that day. I tried the Heimlich. I tried mouth to muzzle. No go. He was dead, dead, dead. I killed the best friend a boy could ever have." Bob knuckles an incipient sniffle away, stifles a sob. "I haven't had another friend since. I don't deserve one."

"There, there," we say, our heart rending. "Don't be so hard on yourself. Everyone deserves friendship."

"Yeah?" Bob says. "How many friends you got?"

"We have had a certain number of friends in our past," we assure him. "At present we are far too busy to make new ones."

Bob nods. "Kids don't like to hang with me either."

"Children can be cruel," we say compassionately.

"Children can be dick-heads."

"They make fun of your superior intelligence, no doubt."

"They pick their noses in awe at my intelligence, Bob. I make fun of their stupidity. Jesus, they're so incredibly dull, I can barely stand to talk to them. Got no adult friends either, since I usually intimidate adults who are used to dealing with incredibly stupid kids. They don't know how to act with me when they finally figure out that I'm smarter now than they can ever hope to be. So adults tend to ignore me, hoping I'll go away."

He smiles faintly but (we like to think) fondly at us, enough for us to realize for the first time that he wears braces on his teeth. "I gotta admit, Bob, you're paying me way more attention than the average adult who's not being paid to pay attention to me."

"We are nothing if not attentive."

"But let's not turn this into an afternoon children's special, Bob, young friendless punk genius and eccentric neighborhood codger team up for fun, friendship, and laughs. Let's get back to your problem. You're using a healthy percentage of your brain, is my guess, Bob. You ain't no genius, but you got this incredibly rare focus, this call thing of yours, not to mention this *we* thing, which I'll get to sooner or later, I guess. Problem is, you're focusing on the wrong point."

"What's the point?" we say.

"Good question, Bob. I'll study it and let you know tomorrow. Meantime, I gotta split."

"What about your pizza?"

"No time. My parents will be home any minute, and if I'm not home first, they'll fire the sitter and I'll have to train a new one. Put the pie in the fridge," Bob says on his way out our door. "I'll see you for breakfast."

Minutes after he's left, our intercom buzzes. We let in a laughing, athletically curvaceous, dimple-cheeked girl of seventeen or eighteen wearing a backwards red baseball cap on her pony-tailed head. "Doofussy neighborhood you live in," she tells us, her laughter weakening to a chuckle when we open our door. She hands us a warm and soggy box when we've paid her. "Some kid on a ten-speed

was so busy staring at me, he crashed into a line of garbage cans."
She flips her cap brim forward, fluffs her mussed tail with both
hands, perky young breasts rising. "You'd think he never saw a pizza
before," she says.

cloister-lude

Bob arrives at our door the following morning, ravenous. "Where's that pie?" he says, bee-lining his way toward our galley kitchen and opening the refrigerator. He wears baggy black shorts and over-sized sweatshirt today, black hood obscuring his profile as he stands at our galley kitchen sink, teeth tearing at a slice of cold pizza.

"We could heat that for you in our microwave."

"I like a cold breakfast. Don't even mention oatmeal to me or I'll puke."

We refrain from mentioning our own breakfast, prepared and consumed, neither pleasing nor dis-, several hours earlier.

"Shouldn't you be at school?"

"I told you I was home-schooled."

"Shouldn't you be home, schooling?"

"I *was* home schooled. I passed last year. I got a class to teach this afternoon, though, out at the university. I'm an adjunct, which means no benefits. End of this semester, I'm telling them it's an endowed chair or it's bye-bye Bob. Hey, did you check out that pizza-delivery chick yesterday?" he says, staring at our windowless wall. "What a babe. Order us another pie, Bob, PDQ. I gotta meet her."

"We've been thinking," we begin.

"Keep it up, Bob, only do it quietly, could you? I'm still thinking too. Gimme a minute and I'll have your problem hammered."

We return to our sofa, sit, and watch Bob think. He devours seven-eighths of the large triple-cheese pie, rhythmically chewing in apparently deep rumination, before turning our way and, cowled eyebrows raised, offering us the final slice.

"C'mon, it's good," he says when we politely decline.

"Not for us."

"Take it, Bob," he says and, despite our protestations, deposits the sodden slice limply in our hands. "Brain food," he says, wiping greasy fingers on sweatshirt. He flips back his hood, smiles brilliantly at us. Bits of pizza dough and sauce cling to his braces. "Like the new do?" he says.

"We thought there was something different about you."

He smoothes both hands from shaved temples to back of shaved neck, fingers delicately lingering at shoulder-length braid of blond hair sprouting from crown of head. "Did it myself last night," he says proudly. "It's a bitch getting the back, though, I'll tell you. Takes two mirrors and your head blocks your line of vision. Not to even *mention* a major case of reflective dyslexia. You'd think my dad would be happy, right?" He shakes his head tiredly. "Think again, Bob. Plus my mom's like, 'Are you *sure* you read all the precautions on the hair-coloring bottle? These products are full of carcinogens, honey.' I'm like, '*Duh*, Mom.' I invented my own hair dye, actually. Did a little research and mixed it up myself. Perfectly safe and effective. You'd be surprised what you can make using chemicals commonly found in kitchen-sink cabinets. I would've filed for a patent last night, but I was too busy working on *your* problem."

"You did all that last night?"

"I don't sleep much. Anyway, your problem's solved, Bob. I got one word for you."

We ask.

"Cloister-ROM," Bob says, "with a capital ROM."

"Meaning?"

"Cybercephalically-looped-ontologically-interposed-solipsistic-thought-enhancing-receptor—Read Only Memory."

"Meaning?"

"Meaning I gave your problem some good thought, Bob, and I can't figure out any reason why the kind of call you're talking about shouldn't take place."

"Thank you," we say. "You have sauce on your chin."

Distended tongue reaching just short of the sauce's splotch, Bob shrugs and wipes his mouth on his sleeve. "It's gonna take some tinkering," he says, "but I roughed out a system guaranteed to get you *some* kind of special call, and the beauty of it is, all it'll take is you, your Smithsonian here, and a few odds and ends I can pick up cheap at garage sales."

"What kind of system?" we say suspiciously.

"You gotta trust me on that, Bob. It's pretty radical. You'll be tempted to call me crazy when I tell you about it. I'm warning you right now not to. People at MicroMac called me crazy when I said I could revamp a pocket calculator so it would handle the payroll demands of their whole operation worldwide. They're the crazy ones. They don't *want* to make a cheaper, more efficient, more specialized thinking machine—there's no profit in it. That's why pharmaceutical companies keep coming out with a skabillion different hypertension medications that basically do the same thing, instead of working on a cure for Culley's Syndrome, for instance."

"What's Culley's Syndrome?"

"Onset of almost total paralysis coinciding with this one girl's very first menstrual period," Bob says, blushingly stumbling over the pronunciation of 'menstrual.' "She's the only person with the syndrome, so they named it after her. But nobody's working on it 'cause there's no money in it. I ran across a paper on it in *The New England Journal of Medicine* when I was researching a home remedy for this plantar's wart I got growing out of my instep. I just can't get rid of it. It's like this evil, leechy thing produced by my very own skin cells. I feel betrayed every time I step on it. But the system I worked out won't betray you, Bob. You can trust me *much* farther than you can throw me. Do you trust me, Bob?"

"Though we have no logical reason to," we answer truthfully, "we do tend to trust you, Bob."

"'Tend to,' Bob?"

"Almost unequivocally."

"Without reservation, Bob? I'm not a hundred percent sure I can work with you if you have even a smidgenth of a percentage of reservation, Bob."

"Well..."

"You're hedging, Bob. Don't hedge. Tell the truth."

"We *do* have one slight reservation," we say.

"Gimme."

"Despite the increase in otherwise-employable brain cells which the practice affords you," we say, "we still find your habit of calling us 'Bob' somewhat disconcerting, if not outright unseemly. We are, after all, old enough to be your grandfather, and, as such, feel that we should be accorded some modicum of the sort of respect you mentioned your mother mentioning regarding your filial relationship with your father."

"You want me to call you 'Gramps'?"

"Not at all, but the standard honorific—"

"*Mr.* Bob?"

"—preceding our given surname should suffice."

"You never gave me your given surname."

"It's, um, heh-heh, Roberts," we manage.

"First time I've heard you laugh," Bob says, laughing himself. "It's a creaky thing, ain't it? But I'm inspired by it. Hey, I'm young enough to change my M.O. at a moment's notice. You want respect, you got it. Happy now, Mr. Bobs?"

"Approximately."

"Trust me?"

"Totally."

"Good. Lay back on the sofa and relax."

"That would be 'lie back,' Bob, and for what?"

"Gotta do a little brain scan," he says, reaching into his pocket. "Lie yourselves down."

"'Lay' would take the direct object," we say. "What's that?"

"You're equivocating, Mr. Bobs. Don't equivocate. This," he says, gently pushing us back on the sofa with one hand and holding out a black plastic device that resembles a child's walkie-talkie in the other, "is a hand-held magnetic resonance imaging machine. I designed, assembled, and modified it last night. I'll need pictures to figure the best point of entry."

"Entry?"

"To install your jack."

"Our jack?"

"To fit the cable in that connects you to your computer."

"You're joking, we assume."

"Oh, don't worry, I'm going to like totally revamp your computer, too. I wouldn't hook you up as is."

"We don't see how that would be possible."

"Oh, it'd be *possible*, all right, but unless I modify and focus your computer, you'd never get your call. Don't worry, though. I got all the specs right here." Bob taps his shaved temple. "Plus I read up on the brain and microsurgery last night, and I'm guessing I can whip up a killer anesthetic from the dregs of my mom's medicine cabinet."

He passes the walkie-talkie-like device over our forehead, squints at a thumbnail-sized screen on its back.

"Perhaps you had better describe your system to us in a bit more detail," we suggest.

"In layman's terms?"

"Preferably," we say.

Bob continues to scan our brain as, in layman's terms and voice rising excitedly near the end of each lengthening sentence, he explains that the kind of call we are waiting for, since its expectation springs from and is dependent on the brain's concept of 'self,' must, perforce, be generated by the self itself: self-generated and self-received. Positing the source of said message to be the self itself, the content of said message to be the self's ontological reassurance that the self is indeed the self, and the recipient of said message to be, again, the self, one might assume that said message is being transmitted and received ceaselessly, even as we speak, every waking and sleeping moment of every day of our existence. "We're talking solipsistic loop here, Mr. Bobs," Bob assures us. "Like your brain's sending this constant message to itself saying, 'Hey, I'm me! Who're you?' And the brain receives the message and transmits back, 'Hey, I'm *me*! Who're *you*?' And the brain receives and transmits etcetera. I'm thinking this may be the basic difference between your intelligent and your unintelligent entities. You know your entities, Mr. Bobs. The unintelligent ones, the ones you probably crunch a lot of, your 'things' as opposed to your 'creatures,' they're basically transmitting, 'Fuck if I know' without the 'I,' of course—excuse my Entitese."

"We wish you wouldn't use the f-word so much," we say. "It's unseemly."

"The fucking f-word's unseemly?" Bob says. "Who knew?" Bob turns off his makeshift MRI machine. "But now we get to the fly in the K-Y," he says. "Like how the *heck* can your self be sending and receiving this message to itself without you yourself—your fully *conscious* self, that is—being in on it? In other words, you're *getting* your call, dude. You just don't *hear* it."

Which fly in said personal lubricant all comes down to the old split-brain syndrome, Bob explains, "a problem any surgeon worth his or her value in real estate could take the knife to and solve in a Pakistani minute. Left hemisphere, right hemisphere, a snip here, a suture there, and voila, east meets west and your brain's communicating with itself out loud non-stop, and boy-oh-boy do you know it, Mr. Bobs. Unfortunately, you yourself are drooling down the front of your straitjacket while this communication ensues."

Which brings us, Bob explains, to Bob's particular stroke of genius, if he doesn't mind saying so himself.

"Simple," he says. "We just splice into the loop, feed the message into an *outside* intelligence (that'd be your computer, once I revamp it), which translates the message into its own code (I'm working on it, trust me) and, after a nano-second's delay, reads the message back into the loop, where the brain will have to accept it as a brand new message transmitted from an *outside* source and, in order to understand it, *translate* it. It may take awhile for the brain to accomplish this, but so long as you're in the loop, the brain'll be actively working on it. Sooner or later, you get your 'call,' Mr. Bobs."

"Perhaps you'd better explain again."

Bob sighs, shakes his head, suddenly snaps his fingers. "You ever get a feeling of deja vu, Mr. Bobs?"

"We think we almost remember such a feeling."

"That's what your call should feel like at first, this feeling you can't quite put your finger on. Only instead of being a fleeting feeling you never quite catch up with before it's gone, *this* feeling will stick with you as long as you're hooked up, giving your mind *plenty* of time to not only catch up to it but tackle it, pin it to the ground, and tickle it till it says 'uncle' loud and clear. All I have to do," he says, laying aside the MRI, "is install a jack," he says, forefinger suspended between our eyes, "right about here."

His finger touches our forehead. The nape of our neck crawls.

"Say the word, Mr. Bobs, and I'll start right in."

We meet his smiling gaze.

"Are you absolutely convinced," we say, rising from our back, "that everything you've just explained to us is true?"

"Ninety-nine-point-nine-nine-nine percent positive," Bob says.

We smile back. "Then you *must* be crazy," we say.

"Crazy?" Bob says, smile fading. "*Crazy,*" he says, voice turning to a snarl.

"We only meant—"

"*I'll* show you *crazy!*" Bob shouts, and, fumbling with belt buckle beneath hem of baggy sweatshirt, he whirls away from us, drops his shorts, bends over, and, naked bottom thrust usward, farts explosively. "I got your crazy for you right here!" Bob rages. He runs to our galley kitchen tool drawer, pulls out a certain ex-spouse's second anniversary present to us, and, knobby elbow pumping like a piston, methodically wields ball-peen hammer across the length and breadth of our hard drive's chassis.

"There," he pants when he's finished. "My work here is done."

"Does this mean you won't be helping us receive our call?" we say.

"Your call, your call, your call," Bob says. "What about my pizza? Gimme!" He grabs the slumping slice from our hands (thus reminding us that we've been holding it all the while) and stuffs it into his mouth whole. He tries to speak while chewing, waves off our polite protestations that we can't understand a word he's saying, swallows with difficulty. "You think *I'm* crazy," he says, spraying flecks of pizza, "you oughta take a look at your*selves* sometime!" He turns for the door, slams it open. "I'm outa here, Bobs," he says. "Go fuck yourselves."

We get up to close the door behind him and, not entirely unabashedly, exit our apartment for the first time in recent memory. We lean over stairwell's railing, watch blond ponytail bob as Bob gallops groundward. "We meant to tell you," we call down after him. "Rub a cut potato on that wart."

"As if!" Bob calls back.

We close our door, latch it, return to our sofa, stare at the ceiling. Our fingers are sticky with sauce from the pizza. We put a finger to our mouth, lick it experimentally.

We do not think we have ever tasted anything quite so terrible in all our lives.

stunner-rom

S orry about my twin brother," the crew-cutted boy announces when we open our door to him the next afternoon. "He gets pretty touchy sometimes. I have to admit, he was a bear to live with when he got home. I stayed out of his way as much as possible, but at dinner my father said, 'What bug flew up *your* butt, young man?' My brother, surly as usual, answered, 'Musta been a *butt*-erfly, Pops.' Dad looked at him sternly, but then my mother began to giggle, my father relented and laughed as well, and so before you know it the tension had subsided, and my twin was back to his normal, happy self again. That's when he told me all about your problem, and I must admit I'm intrigued. Mind if I come in, Mr. Bobs?"

We let the young man in, and he introduces himself as Bob too or two, homophonics obscuring literal meaning.

"Would that be Bob 'also' or Bob 'numeral two'?" we ask.

"Exactly, but you don't have to call me that if you don't want to, Mr. Bobs. You don't mind me calling you Mr. Bobs, Mr. Bobs, do you? Bob's told me so much about you that I almost feel we know each other. Have you ever gotten a feeling of deja vu when you've just met a person?"

"Didn't you just ask us that?"

"Ba-dum-bump," Bob's twin says, drumming the palms of his hands on our galley kitchen countertop. "After my brother felt more like himself again last night, he went back to the drawing board on your problem, and he's come up with a whole new plan. He asked me to ask you if you're still game."

"No more Cloister-ROM?" we say.

"Well," he says, somewhat perplexed. "He isn't prepared to reinvent the wheel here, Mr. Bobs. There will be *some* kind of ROM, but I talked with him, and he's agreed to modify the loop some."

"Why?"

"Why modify the loop?"

"Why the necessity for ROM? We're no computer expert, but doesn't ROM require some sort of compact disk to play?"

Bob's twin smiles indulgently. "In a manner of speaking, Mr. Bobs, *you* are the CD, or rather your brain is. The computer is enabled to execute read-only commands. You wouldn't want to be hooked up to a machine that could *write* on your brain, would you?"

"We haven't the faintest. Wouldn't you?"

"You wouldn't," Bob's twin answers soberly. "Write permissions should be zealously guarded. With Cloister-ROM, your computer has permission to read your brain's message and read the same message verbatim back into the loop. God only knows what sort of damage could be done with a program enabled with write permissions." Bob's twin grimaces, closes his eyes for a moment, softly taps index finger on lower lip. "Anyway, we've discussed an alternative approach, Bob and I, and this one involves—" he grimaces slightly "—virtual rather than actual computer-brain hook-up."

"Meaning?"

"Meaning my brother, in his passion for and familiarity with machines, often fails to take into account the subtle tolerances involved in human engineering."

"Again?"

"No surgery this time, Mr. Bobs. We promise."

"Who's we?"

"My twin and I in this case, Mr. Bobs," he chuckles, "though after today I'll be working in an invisible consultant capacity only. Can you, will you, accept our help?"

"Can you, will you, help us, Bob?"

The boy smiles. "My brother said to tell you under one condition."

"And that condition would be?"

"He wrote it down. I'll read it to you later. I haven't much time, and I wanted to get right to work fixing the computer my brother told me he ball-pinged near to extinction. Just between you and I, that smashing thing last night was mostly for dramatic effect. My brother has way too much respect for machinery to simply destroy it. Actually, he was simply beginning the modification procedure that I'll be finishing today. The hard drive's memory has to be cleared to make room for neural net initialization. Why are you looking at me funny?"

"'Between you and me,'" we answer absently. "Your hair."

"Like it?"

"We had meant to mention it when first you arrived."

"My father gave me this haircut last night after dinner. He called it a Parris Island Pompadour, heh-heh." Bob's twin runs a hand over the crown of his close-cropped bristles. "My brother, in his usual witty manner, laconically commented, 'You get a number tattooed on your wrist with that?' Peculiarly enough, though, he found 'the gulag style,' as he called it, rather 'tight,' even though my father certainly never intended it to be anything but utilitarianly short. I suspect Bob will be following my tonsorial lead soon enough. There's lots less stuff on your mind when you're hairless."

We buff a palm over our own long-bald cranium. "We've barely ever given it a thought."

"Precisely. Plus, hey—that is to say—apropos of nothing—but re that potato remedy for warts you told Bob about, about which you told Bob, excuse my dangling prep etcetera. Where did you come up with that?"

"We can't recall. But we're positive it works."

"All the medical literature recommends salicylic acid or cryostatic excision via liquid nitrogen."

"So?"

Bob's twin shudders. "Bob is scared to death of liquid nitrogen."

We shrug.

"He tried the acid route every day for a month. It left a particularly debilitating, ghastly white, necrotized hole in his foot that a new—out of which a new wart grew."

"You have an impressive working vocabulary for a child your age," we observe.

"I have an impressive working vocabulary for somebody *any* age," he says, "and you ain't heard a tenth of it yet."

"Tell him to try the potato," we say. "Trust us."

Bob's twin purses his lips. Braces sparkle dully within. "Do you have any children of your own?" he says.

"Multitudes."

"Would you give one of them the same advice?"

"Certainly, if any one of them ever called and asked. Unfortunately, none of them ever call."

"Phone lines go both ways, Mr. Bobs. Sometimes you have to make that call yourself. And speaking of calls, let me get to work on the first step in facilitating yours."

This particular Bob has brought his own tool kit. He opens it, pulls out screwdriver and roll of duct tape, and gets right to work on our computer.

"Should we order you a pizza?" we say.

He looks at his watch. "Wait a few," he says. "I want to make sure that pizza delivery person Bob mentioned is on call. He claims she's quite a looker. Tell me honestly, Mr. Bobs, do you think a girl her age could get interested in a boy Bob's age?"

"No," we say.

"What the fuck," he says. "Make the call now."

"Eh-eh-eh," we remind him.

"Eh-eh-eh what, Mr. Bobs?"

"Unseemly language."

"Oh," Bob's twin says. He smiles slyly. "Fucking oops," he amends.

When the intercom buzzes, Bob's twin takes a break from working on our computer and we from staring at our ceiling to answer it.

"Pizza," a young and feminine voice says.

We buzz up the self-same delivery person that Bob and his twin have been waiting for most of their lives.

She peers around me as I pay her, catches Bob's twin furtively scrutinizing her every move, and laughs aloud, head tilted back, breasts jiggling nubilely beneath thin red Pizza Hut t-shirt with each chuckling exhalation. Bob's twin blushes to the crown of his buzz-cut head.

She winks in his direction. "What are you looking at?" she asks him.

"Nothing," he mumbles.

"Wrong answer," she says.

"Rather cute," we say when she's gone.

"Except for looking at me funny. Why do all the pizza delivery girls look at me funny? What, do I have like extra noses where my zits should be or something?"

"No," we assure him.

"That's good. She probably just thought I was my twin brother. Happens all the time. Anyway, I have to get home. I have this relationship with the babysitter."

"Arrangement, you mean?"

"Arrangement," he says. "It's mortifying."

"We'll put the pizza in our refrigerator."

"For my brother," he says. "My work here is done."

"What about your brother's one condition?"

He slaps his skull sharply. "Almost forgot. He would've killed me." He rummages in his tool kit, gives us an envelope with our names block-printed across the front, then heads for the door. "I'll just leave the tools here," he says. "My brother will see you tomorrow. Meantime, you have a pleasant or at least not especially unpleasant evening, Mr. Bobs. It was nice meeting you."

And Bob's twin brother walks out our door, never to return.

"BTW," he yells up the stairwell as we're locking our door. "Keep your computer running, and don't use it for anything. It's nurturing a neural net even as we speak."

Later in the evening, after we have finished staring at our ceiling for a time, listening to the soft hum of our computer in the hush of our darkened efficiency, we open the envelope to discover a sort of poem:

"Can You, Will You, Help Us, Bob?"
by Bob
I cannot, will not, help you, Bob,
I cannot help you with this job;
I cannot help you get your call,
I cannot help you, not at all,
Until you 1st shed verbal truss,
1st-person, plural, Bobs-R-Us.
I have a plan—it's neat and sure—
that offers singular allure,
but help from this computer wiz
must come without the plural biz.
I do not like 1st-person, plural:
You must not use it, Lawrence Durell!

"Ouch," we say to ourselves, folding the poem up and tucking it neatly back in its envelope. "Who's Lawrence Durell?"

"A rhymey kinda guy, is all I know," Bob answers the following morning over his breakfast of cold pizza, crew-cut head bobbing rhythmically to the tempo of his teeth. "Bottom line: You want my help, you gotta lose the 'we'."

"But we have been referring to ourselves as ourselves most of our lives now," we say.

"I don't care. It sounds stupid."

"But why?"

"Because."

"Because why?"

"Just because. Listen to yourself for a sec. I mean, it's kinda cool at first—different, anyway—but after awhile it gets old. Belabored. Attenuated. Ridiculous. Idiotic."

"Story of our lives," we say experimentally, listening to ourselves. We close our eyes for better concentration. "Our lives seem belabored and attenuated to us," we say. "Sometimes we cannot stand to hear ourselves speak, we sound so ridiculously idiotic. Perhaps we have, in fact, been sounding stupid to others all our lives now." We open our eyes, and suddenly it hits us.

"We pause now for an epiphany," Bob says.

"You're right!" we exclaim. "It *does* sound stupid."

"Bingo. So knock it off, why don't you?"

"We're not at all sure it will prove to be quite so easy."

"Easy shmeezy. Call up your word-search file. Delete 'we'. Replace with 'I'. Simple."

"We can't do it," we say.

"'I can't do it,' you mean. Say it, Bob."

"'I can't do it,'" we say, brow furrowing with the effort.

"Good. Now get rid of those mental quotation marks I'm sensing with my seventh sense (which just goes to show you what a higher percentage of active brain cells can achieve, punctuation having a certain discernible atomic weight all its own) and try it again. You sound like a parrot."

"Can we stop this, please?"

"Who's we, Bob?"

"You and me, Bob," we say, voice logy with fatigued confusion.

"That being you and I, Bob?"

"Yes, the nominative case, of course, you and I," I say. "I must have been mistaken."

"By George," Bob says, "I think we've got it. Violins swell, French horns blare, timpani rumbles. How's it feel, Bob?"

"Different," I say.

"Simple, wasn't it?"

I reach deep into myself for the answer. There's so much extra space there now. "I don't know," I say. "Relatively, I suppose."

"Good," Bob says. "Now I can *really* go to work."

"Really?" I say. *I* say. I *say*. I say *I say* for the first time in longer than I care to remember, hoping beyond hope. "You'll work on getting me my call?"

"If I have to make it myself," Bob says. "But I won't have to once I get your brand-spanking-new neural net up and running. Don't worry, Bob, I got the whole thing dicked in my head."

"Better get it down on paper," I chide, jokingly. I jokingly chide, another first. "And what, may I ask, happened to *Mr.*?"

"He went the way of that plural dude, Bob."

•

"Please," I object several times in the days that follow, "you have to let me pay you for your work."

"Just keep the pizza coming, Bob. (Not to mention that yummy pizza girl. BTW, what'd my socially-challenged twin brother say to her? She looks at me like I'm Geekatroid Nerdsterwitz! Story of my life.) That'll be payment enough. That and petty cash for scrounged parts, which I'm itemizing (and which so far is running cheaper than pizza, you big tipper, you). That and your undying gratitude. That and listening to me talk. Nobody ever listens to me talk, did I mention? Everybody just sorta gets this glassy eyed look after maybe thirty seconds and then they find the first opportunity to tell me they'd love to chat but they got something like ex*treme*ly crucial to do. That's why I like you, Bob. You listen like you *never* have anything crucial to do."

"Well, there are my entities, of course, but crunching them has never felt particularly crucial. In fact, I haven't practiced my livelihood since before we met, and now that you've taken over my computer, I fear I may have lost my job."

"Another good reason to let me work for you gratis. You got hungry ex-spouses and offspring to feed. You OK in that department, BTW?"

"I have certain investments that should carry me for awhile."

"Good. After I'm done with this project, we'll get to work on retraining you for a new career. I'm thinking security guard at a museum or night-shift convenience store clerk. You have that look. Plus hey! Did I tell you? I think your spud trick's working. I tried it the past few days and I'm noticing some definite wart shrinkage. I don't get it. No *way* a potato should have any effect on the wart virus. But there you go. Sometimes you just need a little faith for the magic to work—hint, hint, Bob. And speaking of work, let me get back to it. My sitter's on the rag again, and she wants me home early. Been cutting it close lately, and she's afraid of losing her phony baloney job."

"Why are you doing all this?" I ask in wonder.

"Doing all what, Bob?"

"Planning, inventing, assembling, all this work. What's in it for you?"

"Well, *duh*," he says. "I'm doing it 'cause it's *fun*. Why *else* would I be doing it, Bob?"

Each day Bob brings cardboard boxes full of scavenged equipment—an old DVD player, several broken laptops, a pair of over-sized headphones, a first-generation X-box, an ancient Atari joystick, boxload upon boxload of jumbled wiring, coaxial cables, circuits, fiberoptics, chips (all "Smithsonian relics," he assures me, all "dirt cheap"), and a single battered welder's mask with opaque visor—until my galley kitchen countertop begins to resemble a flea market's bargain bin, and I must set dishware and cutlery atop microwave oven in order to take my standing meals. Bob works with a kind of serenely efficient and focused attention that belies his almost constant stream of trivial chatter. When he isn't putting together some unearthly-looking component at my countertop, the odor of soldering compound singeing my nostrils, Bob is installing said component at my work station, a rococo assemblage of wires and dubious paraphernalia he keeps imperfectly concealed beneath my plastic daisy-motif shower curtain at all times, even when he's working on it. "Because it's a surprise," he explains when he makes me promise never to peek beneath the curtain. "If you'd get out and spend an hour or two in a nice dark cineplex or something, I wouldn't *have* to work like this," he insists, ducking out from under sheath, wringing wet with perspiration and gasping for air. "I know, I know, you'd prefer not to," he complains when I confess my nearly absolute reluctance to leave my once-tidy efficiency despite the almost overwhelming guilt I feel at the sight of him working under such unhealthful conditions for a boy his age, "but the less you know, the better. If you can't leave, then keep your eyes closed. Or keep an eye on that ceiling some more. I think I saw it move."

•

Several weeks pass, and I begin to experience grave misgivings. Bob has grown unusually quiet in recent days and appears rather wan, almost forlorn. He no longer flaps out from beneath his shower curtain when the pizza is delivered (remaining burrowed even after his delivery girl audibly asks, "What happened to that cute little boy of yours?" on her recentest visit), and he no longer devours the entire pie (desultorily picking at a slice or two and leaving the rest to accumulate in my pizza-box-burdened refrigerator). He seems to have lost weight: dark circles rim his squinting eyes; his face, topped by the rough and patchy new growth of his crew cut, looks drawn and haggard. And I begin to question my *own* motives. Do I truly believe that this poor boy is capable of perfecting a machine that will get me my call? Do I believe that such a call, a call a certain "we" claimed to have waited all his "lives" for, truly exists? Could "our" call be simple vanity? After all, why should *my* life prove to be "indescribably delicious" if, in order to make it become so, I must watch this boy lose the taste for his own?

"It's not fun anymore," I say to him one day. "I can tell."

"There's fun and there's fun," Bob says, head bobbing beneath plastic curtain. "This is a lot harder than I figured, is all. You don't just click your magic heels together three times and say, 'Gimme a call, gimme a call,' you know."

"Then quit," I say. "Please."

Bob ducks out from under the curtain, wipes sweat from his brow, astonished.

"I'm *this* close," he says, forefinger hovering a millimeter from thumb, tears suddenly welling, "and you're losing confidence in me?"

"I'm losing confidence in myself," I say. "Perhaps there is no call."

"There's a call, all right," he says gruffly. He paws at a tear that has spilled over the baggy lower lid of one eye and run a course down his cheek. "And I'm ninety-nine-point-nine-nine-nine percent positive that this machine will put it through to you, once I get the fucking thing running right."

"Excuse your French."

"All I gotta do is dot the t's and cross the i's," he pouts.

"I'm concerned for you," I say. "You haven't been looking at all well lately."

"You and my parents should meet," Bob says sullenly. "'Don't get your hopes up too high, son. You're just a boy, after all. You need your sleep. There's plenty of time to invent all *sorts* of wonderful inventions.'" He rolls his eyes wearily. "I'm telling you there's a call, Bob. I'm positive of that."

"But how can you be so sure?"

"Educated guess," he says, and then smiles softly. "It's like this, Bob. Say you get in a spaceship and you travel to a singularity—a black hole, it's called—and, gravity being what it is, you're caught and pulled into the singularity's event horizon, where, by all laws of physics, you'll be trapped and pulled at the speed of light right into the heart of this black hole, which is the densest, blackest heart in the whole universe, where matter is packed so tightly nothing can ever escape. So you're caught, OK? Just into the event horizon, ready for the big plunge. But relativity being what it is and isn't, time sorta comes to a dead standstill at the event horizon, so (this would work a lot better if you spoke math) you can be said to be existing there in no time, which means you're existing there forever with everything else that makes up the singularity, and (granting consciousness, just for argument's sake) get this, you suddenly *know* everything there is to know about that singularity, because it's *you* now, see? and you're *it*. So OK. Off to your right (heh-heh, even the *math* can't do *this*) there's a couple of entities (your ears should perk up *now*, Bob) from the Planet Grrdjgzrg (don't ask me to spell it), just a couple of blobs of amorphous hyperplasm, just floating along, 'face' to 'face', like mirror images, perfectly parallel, perfectly symmetrical, one spinning clockwise, the other counter- (and you know all this for a *fact* since 'you' are part of the same singularity 'they' are—keep up with me now, Bob), and there's this single thread of sub-particular energy connecting the exact center of one Grrdjgzrgian (that hurts the *throat*, man, shoulda just called them blobs of Bob) to the precise center of the other, this thread of energy just undulating between them as they spin in perfect unison forever and ever or until the next Big Bang, whichever comes first, amen. Exam bonus question number one: What are they doing?"

"Me?" I say.

"No other students in attendance, Bob."

"I don't know."

"Guess."

"I wouldn't know how to begin."

"That's the difference between you and me, Bob," Bob says. "I can guess *exactly* what they're doing."

"Yes?"

"Shit, yeah. They're playing gin rummy."

I think this over. "I don't get it," I say.

"Sure you do," Bob says. "Or you *could*, if you'd just take an educated guess."

"But how do you know they're playing gin rummy?"

"I told you. Educated guess. You're part of the singularity, remember?"

"But why would they be playing gin rummy?"

"Fuck if I know," he says, winking. "What *else* are they supposed to do?"

•

Then one morning Bob arrives, spends an hour or so making minor adjustments beneath the strangely listless shower curtain, and comes up for air to inform me that his work is, for now, essentially finished. "I'm just waiting for a UPS delivery of this final special part I had to order," he says, clearing the galley kitchen countertop of the dregs of his enterprise, boxing spare parts, dropping loose nuts and bolts into his baggy pants pockets. "Couldn't find one at any of the rummage sales I went to, no big surprise. It's pretty specialized." He ducks his head, suppresses a grin, a slight rosy hue rising in what has lately been a pallid complexion. "I found it in one of my dad's catalogues.

Used one of my mom's credit cards, which, by the way, I got to bill you for before she gets *her* bill."

"Let me write you a check."

"No rush," he says, waving me off. "I'll get it before I leave. But I'm pretty pissed off it's not here already. I ordered it 'Rush Delivery' way last week, and I gave 'em your address, so it should've been here by now. Meantime, I got my thumb up my ass with nothing to do. Feel like going for a walk or something? I gotta get out of this tomb."

"I'd rather you show me what you've been working on all this time," I say.

"It's not finished."

"A single part," I say. "Show me. I can fill in the blank."

He eyes me guardedly. "I don't think so, Bob."

"Why not?"

"You're not ready yet."

I shrug. "I'm as ready as I'll ever be."

He considers this. "When's the last time you left this apartment?" he asks.

"It's been ages," I say. "I have my groceries delivered, you know. I haven't gone out since well back in my plural days."

"Any particular reason not to?"

"No, no particular reason not to—I've been outside in the past— but no compelling reason to, either. I simply don't *care* to."

Bob tilts his head back, appraises me like a stud poker player. "I'll make you a deal, Bob," he says. "You go for a walk with me, let me air you out a little, and I'll show you the machine when we get back. What say, Bob? I'm dying here."

I consider this. "I'll make *you* a deal," I counter. "Show me the machine first."

"Real estate agent's another option for mid-life career change, Bob," he says. "OK, deal. It's not much to *look* at, understand, but this baby's gonna do the job." Bob moves to the work station, grabs two fistfuls of plastic daisies, hesitates. "Pay no attention to the mess behind the curtain!" he announces like a carnival barker, and then, lifting and snapping his wrists so the curtain flutters up and off to land on the sofa with a crackle of static, "Voila!" he cries. He stands staring at his own creation. "Cool, huh?" he manages, finally.

"Cool," I echo.

"OK," Bob says, "let's hit the road."

"Wait," I say, circling to inspect it. As far as I can tell, it is my old computer, ripped open at the seams, gutted and stuffed with tier upon tier of stacked office in-baskets, each overflowing with an intricate maze of memory chips, the whole construction open to the air. Wires run from tier to near-toppling tier. Monitor screen has been removed, and a bundle of wires snake from the rear of its empty shell, connecting to the welder's mask lying atop it, hood and visor sprouting more wiring like a colander of tangled spaghetti. A long Velcro strap has been sewn chest-high to the back of my swivel chair, and on the seat itself rests the joystick, connected to computer by cable. Another cable, several feet long and leading to the base of the joystick, dangles its unconnected end from chair to floor.

It looks, for all the world, like the Erector Set concoction of a madman's troubled child.

I bend down, the machine humming like a whisper in my ear, reach to touch cable's pronged tip, stop. I look up at Bob.

"That's OK," he says. "No juice yet. That's where the special part goes."

I nod. "What exactly *is* this machine?"

"I got one word for you," Bob says. "Stunner-ROM."

"Meaning?"

Bob scratches his fuzzy head, nervously jingles a pocketful of metal screws. "It's been awhile," he says. "Got it right on the tip of my tongue. Oh, yeah. Solipsistic-thought-uploaded-to-neural-net-for-electronic-reception," he says. "Something like that, anyway. It's tough coming up with snappy acronyms for all my inventions. Let's hit it."

"But how does it work?" I say.

Bob taps his foot. "You got a couple years?"

"Yes."

"Short and sweet, your Stunner's built around a neural network computer, a basic brain programmed to process and systematize new bits of information through trial and error learning. It can receive, learn, and transmit. What I plan to do with this is something like what I planned to do with the Cloister-ROM, only here we're talking strictly virtual as opposed to *actual* connection with your brain. You wear this thing," he says, pointing to the welder's mask, "which picks up your brain waves, feeds them to the neural net, and, after a nanosecond's pause for reorganization, the neural net beams 'em back to the mask, where you virtually receive 'em. Deja vu all over again."

He gnaws at a thumbnail savagely, glances at the door. I notice dark smudges on his chin and at the corners of his upper lip.

"You ready to go now?" he says.

"What's the joystick for?"

"There's some spatial considerations on the virtual end. You'll see."

"And this?" I say, picking up the loose cable connection.

"I told you, that's where the part we're waiting for goes."

"And what does that part do?"

"I gotta tell you, Bob," he says, "I'm feeling like a rat in a rat trap here. I'll explain the whole thing once it's all put together. Meantime, though, if I don't get out of this fucking apartment right now, I'm gonna start gnawing off my own foot. Do you mind? I *showed* it to you already. Could we just split this place now, huh, could we, please?"

"Of course," I say, and I stand and follow him to the door. "I feel as though I'm forgetting something."

"Keys?"

"Oh, yes. Where would those be?" I wonder. "Do I need a jacket? Perhaps I should change into some street shoes." Suddenly, the enormity of my decision looms like a mountain, blocking my vision.

"Come on," Bob says. "I'll take care of you."

And he does. Finding keys, light windbreaker, and pair of tasseled loafers for me, he ushers me out the door, hand on my elbow, like a boy scout earning today's civic merit badge. The door lock clicks behind me as the stairwell steepens vertiginously below.

"Take it easy," Bob whispers beside me. "I won't let you fall. Look," he says as he opens the lobby door for me, "I don't mean to blow off all your questions or anything, but what I'm working on is pretty heady stuff, you know? I just hate explaining everything I'm doing all the time. People get hung up on the simplest things, when all you really have to do is trust the technology."

We step out my building's front door to the sidewalk. Compared to my efficiency's 60-watt bulbs, the brightness of the street is a painful, searing thing, even on an overcast day with the sun hidden behind a bank of tall buildings. I take a misstep, stagger.

"Hey!" Bob says, supporting me. He reaches into his pocket. "Here, wear my shades," he says. "I don't need them."

I don a pair of red-framed sunglasses with a single mirrored lens running from temple to temple. The world darkens somewhat.

"They're you," Bob says, ambling me down the street. "But soon as I say 'trust the technology,' I'm immediately like, 'Sure thing, Dr. Frankenstein!' You know, like maybe I'm messing too much with good old Mother Nature's plan, so why *should* you trust me, right? And it sure as hell doesn't help, working in that tomby, crypty, windowless coffin of a room you got up there, with you looking like Herman Munster on chemo and everything. You ever try Rogaine?"

"No."

"Having a good time?"

"Approximately. Can we go back now?"

Bob laughs. "I'm taking you for a run in the park, Bob. Did you know you got one of the nicest parks in town just down the street from you?"

"I vaguely recall. You have a smudge of what I think might be pencil graphite on your chin."

"I only use a pen," Bob says. "No mistakes." He touches his chin. "That's a goatee I'm growing. Mustache too. What do you think?"

"Aren't you rather young for facial hair?"

"I'll be thirteen tomorrow."

"Happy birthday, Bob."

"Tomorrow," he says. "Park's this way."

Bob jaywalks me through a line of cars stopped for a traffic light up the block, weaves me around a trio of elderly ladies pushing grocery carts slowly toward us. "Geez, block the whole sidewalk, why don't you?" Bob mutters as we pass.

One of the ladies hears him and glares sharply over her shoulder at me. I smile, move a hand to tip a hat I'm not wearing, continue the motion to smooth back the skin of my scalp. The lady frowns, mutters "Punk," and turns away.

I know this season. I remember it well. I remember this season's weather's subtle seasonal change changing day by day, year after year, this season inexorably changing to the following season, season after season. This season is exactly as I remember it. The air is thick with this season's specific odor, an odor quite a bit riper than my apartment's central air. The temperature of this season is a too-familiar thing, a slurred and boozy temperature that wobbles against the skin like a drunken bum sidestepping a homeward-bound secretary in a crowded subway. The sounds of this season fill my ears, doppler past, squeal in toothless delight, chitter convulsively. This season tastes slightly moldy, a damp bouquet of ferment that I roll across my tongue nostalgically before spitting it dryly into the gutter. Some seasonal changes never change, I think, recalling that this season used to be my favorite, but upon experiencing its offerings once again and matching present experience to what I recall, I recall this season's charms turning suddenly unremarkable one long lost evening, as unenlivening as a moth-flecked streetlight momentarily mistaken for waning moonrise, as disappointing as a childhood record album recovered from attic, dusted off, played for a single uninspiring circuit through scratch and fuzzy buzz, and then returned to attic to collect more dust.

"It's like this, Bob," Bob continues as we pass through the gates of the park. "Far as I'm concerned, everything you need to know happened in *The Wizard of Oz*, and everything *really* important happened at the end. You remember that movie, Bob?"

The park's patrons busy themselves before us, jogging, roller-blading, early picnic lunching; they recline on worn plaid blankets, toss bread crumbs to plucky pigeons, sidestep duck dung down by the pond. A blue-jeaned young mother with sun-streaked brown hair holds a tail-less triangle of kite in both outstretched hands and, despite the absence of breeze, tentatively tosses it skyward, while her dark-eyed adolescent daughter backpedals gamely, a plastic spool of slackening string in each hand. Kite lifts, spins, nosedives earthward. ("*Mo*-om," the daughter pouts gaily, her serious face blossoming with laughter, "throw it *up!*" "I *did*, you little stinker," mother taunts in return. "*You* try it!") The park teems with the aimless excesses of pointless recreation, filled to the brim with lives whose respiteless concerns have nothing to do with me at all.

"Bob?"

"Yes," I answer. "I've seen *The Wizard of Oz*. Many times, back when I was your age."

Bob eyes me dubiously. "How old *are* you, anyway?"

"Take an educated guess."

"Terminal?"

"Not quite that old," I say, watching the kite flutter and fall again.

We stop and stand, Bob's eyes following my line of vision. "They'll never get it launched like that," he says. "There's a thermal down by the pond they could catch, though. Plus, even though they say you don't need one, a little tail would make that thing more aerodynamically active. And speaking of a little tail," he says, "that girl is a *babe!* I wonder how old she is."

"About your age, I'd guess."

"Yeah," he says, eyes clouding. He watches the girl as she switches places with her mother. Her black braid bounces down her sharp-winged back as she leaps athletically, releasing the kite to similar results. "I don't know too many girls my age," he says wistfully. "But anyway," he goes on, recovering and taking my elbow again, though we remain standing where we are, "two important things happen at the end of that movie, the first just a by-the-way thing, BTW, but the second really important to our situation, Bob."

"*Our* situation?"

"Yours and mine, Bob. Don't go plural on me again. The first thing, the by-the-way thing, happens after the phony old wizard hands out the diploma and watch and medal to the straw guy, the metal man, and the scaredy cat, OK? Right before he climbs in the old balloon and takes off without what's-her-name, Bob, that girl from Kansas?"

"Dorothy?"

"Dorothy. There goes another brain cell. So Dorothy's saying her goodbyes, all teary-eyed and all, and she gets to the straw guy, and she hugs him and her voice catches and she says something like, 'Oh! I think I'm going to miss you most of all!' *Right in front of those other two guys, Bob!* You think that tin guy's brand-new heart ain't breaking, hearing her say something like that? I mean, he's standing *right there,* Bob. He *has* to hear her! Plus what's the lion, chopped liver? I don't even *want* to think about the kind of hurt he's feeling deep inside, all scared and lonely and sorry to see her go, and then she comes up with this thoughtless left-handed snub. 'Oh, I had an exciting *time* with you guys, all right, but oh, well, *c'est la fuckin' vie*, I guess I'll get over you two soon enough. The *scare*crow, though, he's a horse of a different color!' That just always really pissed me off, Bob, how that Dorothy bitch could be so cruel. It's like I had this friend once, this one friend I had who used to spend the night at my place lots of times. We'd play these killer marathon games of Monopoly and everything, you know how kids do. So this one Saturday it's raining, so I call up my friend and ask if he can come over, and he says no, his mom told him he can't go anywhere 'cause of the weather and everything, and I say OK and hang up. But then I'm hanging around, bored shitless, and I figure what the hell, it's only rain, so I ride my bike over to his house, knock on the back door like his mom makes all the kids do, and he answers it and right away starts looking at me funny. I'm standing there dripping wet and he's looking at me funny, won't even move out of the doorway to let me in. I say, 'What's up, Bob? Wanna play?' He says, 'I can't, Bob.' I'm like, 'Why not?' He goes, 'Because my mom says I can only have one friend in the house at a time,' and I look behind him, and sure enough there's this other kid, some other kid named Bob, sitting at the kitchen table in front of a game of Monopoly, just fidgeting around all impatient, going, 'Come *on*, Bob, it's your *turn!*' And my friend Bob gives me this like helpless little funny look, like what am I still *standing* there dripping wet in the rain for? So I say, 'Hey, I thought *I* was your friend,' and Bob goes, 'Well, you *are*,' all exasperated like, 'but Eric'—that was that other kid's name, *Eric*, hardly worth burning a brain cell to remember—'but *Eric*,' he goes, '*Eric* is my *best* friend.'"

Bob's jaw clenches; a vein in his temple throbs to the surface: he lets out his breath slowly.

"I'm like, 'Fine,'" Bob grumbles. "'Who needs a fuckin' friend anyway?' (excuse my Munchkin)." He shakes his head sadly. "'Maybe I'll just go home and drown the dog!'" He suddenly breaks into loud, braying laughter, leans into me, shaking with mirth. Mother and daughter pause from their efforts to glance our way.

"I kill myself sometimes," Bob guffaws goofily before convulsing in a severe fit of coughing.

"Are you all right?" I say, supporting his sagging weight.

"Breathed some spit," he manages.

I pound on his back with the heel of my hand.

"Youch!" he cries, teetering away from me. "Not so *hard*, Bob!" He collects himself, wipes his teary eyes. "Nothing traumatic, no big deal," he assures me. "Just something that always got to me in that movie. But the *really* important thing happens after the wizard accidentally flies off in his balloon without Dorothy. Do you remember? That good witch what's-her-name—"

"Don't you think," I uncharacteristically interrupt, "that we might forgo the somewhat tedious (albeit charming) fiction that a young man of your proclaimed intelligence can't spare one measly, niggling brain cell to correctly remember a simple name?"

"Who's we, Bob?"

"You, Bob."

"But this time I really can't remember, I swear. It's like Linda or something but it's not."

"Glenda, isn't it?"

"Glinda, maybe? Anyway," Bob goes on, undaunted, "remember how the good witch bubbles her way in wearing this ballroom gown and cubic zirconium tiara to save the day? She points to the ruby slippers Dorothy's been wearing for like three-quarters of the movie and says how Dorothy's had the power to get back to Kansas all this time and didn't even know it, like as if she's been wasting an hour and a half of screen time with these Oz bozos when all she had to do was click the magic heels together and *zingo*, she'd be beamed back to good old Kansas, which of course she proceeds to do ASAP. But everybody's question is always, 'Shit, Glinda, how come you didn't tell Dorothy that trick back in *Munch*kinland, instead of telling her to follow the yellow brick ucking-fay road, excuse my pig Latin?'

And of course the easy answer is: Because it would have been an effing short movie if Glinda gave up the secret right from the start. Right, Bob? You still with me?"

"I think I understand the dramatic imperatives involved."

"Good. I was worried for a second. Because I got two theories about the *real* answer. First is, the good witch is lying her ass off. Sure, she comes off all wise and kindly and omnipotent in the end, but she needed Dorothy to kill that wicked witch of the *west*, is the *real* state of affairs. And don't tell me old Glinda ain't sweating it for a second, looking cool as a freon cucumber in her glowing chiffon gown. Remember, this Dorothy's a proven witch killer, and Glinda is first and foremost a *witch*, good *or* bad. And Dorothy's got that fiery little squeaky temper, don't forget, especially where her dog's involved. (That'd be Toto, Bob, just to show you I got brain cells to spare.) What do you think might happen if Dorothy somehow discovered she'd been duped by this so-called Good-Witch-of-the-North character, used like a pawn in her grander scheme of things to usurp the power of the sister witches east and west (with no mention of south, I notice), not only putting her*self* into danger, but endangering the life of that little yippy fluff ball who got her into this whole mess in the first place? I don't have to tell you, Bob, old Yolanda must've had her panties in a sweaty bunch waiting for Dorothy to click those heels and split before the truth came out, which, don't get me started thinking about good witch panties, Bob. I'm in a state of constant hormonal flux here, and the results could be mortifying, especially in public."

"As I recall," I muse aloud, "the whole thing was a dream anyway, wasn't it?"

"Yeah, so?"

"So what difference does it make?"

"Just because it's a dream—and that's a big maybe there, Bob, the final black-and-white homecoming scene being left purposely ambiguous in that regard—doesn't mean it doesn't matter. I'm surprised at you."

"Sorry," I say. "What's your second theory?"

"What second theory?"

"Your second theory explaining why Glenda or Glinda doesn't simply tell Dorothy about the power of the ruby slippers when they first meet in Munchkinland?"

"Just testing you, Bob, to see if you were listening. You pass. My second theory is this Wendy witch is *still* lying at the end, or at least she's not telling the whole truth. Hey, she knew the shoes had *power*, sure, but she didn't know you could book flights to Kansas on them. She must've been almost as clueless as Dorothy at the start. Meantime, though, it's her job to *know* these things. She's basically this supernatural problem-solver, and it don't look good for a problem-solver to throw her hands in the air and go 'Fuck if *I* know!' when somebody asks 'em which way to Kansas. So she stalled, is all. Played a hunch, put the kid on the old yellow brick road, bought herself some time to bubble back up north and study the problem in more detail. Soon as she has it all figured out, she bubbles back, gives Dorothy the good news, and fakes like she knew the truth all along. Business as usual, Bob. Play 'em like you got 'em."

"I see," I say, considering this. Mother and daughter continue to giggle, despite their repeated lack of success in getting their kite airborne. They've had several near misses, but still no luck. I find myself admiring their dogged delight in their failures. "And how do these theoretical situations speak to ours?"

"Excuse me?"

"You said that two important things happened at the end of that movie, the second of which (concerning the good witch) was, and I quote, 'really important to our situation, Bob,' end quote."

"Yeah, well, don't quote me on that, Bob," he says, looking around absently. "Sometimes I forget the points of my stories. Hey, you hungry?" he says, reaching in his pocket. "I got a few bucks, and there's a hot dog vendor just up that path there. Do us a couple of dogs, Bob? *Caninus repulsi* smothered in ketchup? Coupla wieners for a coupla weenies? My treat."

"No, thanks."

"Suit yourself, Bob," he says, trotting off toward the path. "Be right back."

I find a bench beneath the kind of grandly aging oak I used to climb when I was a child, and I sit, waiting for Bob's return.

stunner-lude

After a time watching mother and daughter, almost enjoying their unfettered joy myself in a furtively voyeuristic manner, I begin to get an idea. I stand, stretch idly, walk toward them. The daughter is holding the kite now, connected to her mother by forty or so feet of taut string, and so I approach her first.

"Excuse me for interrupting, Miss," I say in a softly unassuming tone, smiling all the while so as not to intimidate her, "but we (that is, my young friend and I, not the royal or plural 'we,' both of which I've eschewed for some weeks now) could not help noticing that your kite might prove more aerodynamically viable were it equipped with a bit of tail, to better take advantage of the pond's thermal updraft, or so my young friend, who should return momentarily with wiener in hand and can better explain said equipage's physics, pointed out not a great while ago. Perhaps we could join you when he returns. It's a perfectly *dandy* day for meeting new people, don't you think?"

The girl's troubled eyes narrow. "Mom?" she calls, but her mother is already running toward us, removing a key-chain from belt loop mid-stride and raising it to her lips. A shrieking whistle blast pierces my ears. The girl falls back, hands covering her own ears, and begins to cry.

"Get *away* from her!" the mother screams, followed by another blast on her whistle.

"Really," I say, taking a step back, hands held palm-forward in placating gesture.

Within reach now, the mother places herself between me and her child and fumbles with her key-chain. She lifts it suddenly and sprays something at my face. I duck and smell an acrid, pepperish odor before the cold spray hits the top of my head. Mother lets loose another shriek from her whistle, the teeth-grinding vibrations of which nearly shatter me back into plurality.

"Help!" she screams. "Somebody help!"

"Please," I say. "Really," I say. "I meant no harm," I say. "Maybe I should just go."

"What's the problem here?" a police officer calls, trotting usward.

"This perv tried to pick up my daughter!" the mother yells.

The child, behind her, hugs her around the waist, weeps against her back.

The officer frowns, gripping my arm firmly.

"No," I say. "I never meant to."

"You'd better come with me, sir," he says. "You too, Ma'am. You can swear out a complaint at the station."

"Dad!" I hear a familiar voice shout in the distance. I turn to see Bob galloping down the path, a hot dog clenched in each windmilling hand.

He arrives, breathless, asks what's going on, quickly and astutely assesses the situation.

Bob explains to the officer that his father has not been at all well lately, ever since the death of his (the boy's, Bob's, my son's) mother only last month, and has in fact been suffering flashback dreams of the three years he (I, his father) spent caged in a secret Afghan mountain cave eating hummus with lice and grubs between regularly scheduled savage beatings…

As he speaks, Bob stoops to the ground, picks up the fallen kite, and idly adjusts one of its plastic crossbars before reaching in his pocket and fastening a bright red bandana to its tail section. The girl, still behind her mother but dry-eyed now, listens to his story with a mixture of awe and standard adolescent incredulity. The mother bites her lower lip and turns sorrowful eyes in my direction. She touches my arm gently, shakes her head in unspoken commiseration.

"So you see, officer," Bob goes on, "this *must* be a complete misunderstanding, although I can understand and totally like *applaud* the lady's protective instincts, es*pecially* when she's protecting such a lovely daughter." Here he smiles shyly at the girl; she rolls her eyes shyly and smiles back. "My father, as you can see, is not a well man at all, but he would *never* harm *any*one, despite his sometimes creepy appearance to the contrary, which as I explained is mostly due to grief and, like, his generation being suckered into waging several loony wars just to fatten a bunch of fat cats' oily wallets, go figure."

As Bob continues to plead the case of his father's feebleminded harmlessness, the officer, hand still on my arm but grip loosened considerably, turns to me, tilts his head, sighs a pleasantly short, snortless sigh through a nose I can see now has been broken at least twice in the past. He cocks a single eyebrow split in half by the scar of some former altercation, and, corner of mouth lifting slightly with amusement, shakes his head briefly, as if to say, "Some kid you got there, Mister," before focusing his tolerant attention back on the boy and his seemingly endless apologia.

I return his smile, though I'm uncertain whether he sees it.

This is the way we fill our days, I think, most of us, anyway, each day presenting us with its own job to do, a job which is, oftentimes, no different from that of the day before or the day before that, but which sometimes offers a twist worth mentioning later at home when the day is through. This officer will fill out the rest of his day now, and then he will punch or log out or off. He will return, then, to the place he spends his nights, a place of rest, he can only hope, a place where he can kick off his tightening shoes, ease the ragged pain trudging up his lower lumbar, wash away the city grit that cakes the deepening creases in his neck, a place where, hopefully, someone waits for him. Be it spouse or lover, father or mother, son or daughter—be it *any* other entity of a certain significance to him who can only imagine what his day's been like, the mountain of pebbled minutiae he's had to stubbornly climb to reach this place—this someone will ask him how his day was.

And what will he say?

Will he tell this someone of the crazy old bald guy and his motor-mouthed boy? How the woman and her daughter shrunk away at first but soon stared in wonder at the prodigy? How he, himself, the officer, lifted a corner of his mouth and slowly shook his head, not so much in awe of the boy's story, an obvious fabrication, but more in gentle indulgence, in doting recollection of the wayward excitation of his own long-gone youth? How just before he arrested the addled geezer—or didn't, as the case by now may have been—the codger creakily returned his smile, sincerely, he could tell, but as though it were his very first smile, a smile he'd been waiting to smile all his life now?

I wonder.

I wonder what sort of soft conclusion this officer might bring his day to later this evening, reclined on sofa before glowing TV screen, perhaps, wearied mind drifting on a sea of sitcom laugh-track, aching feet raised, bedtime toddy in hand, someone's arm, a leg, a softly stirring breast, perhaps, resting warmly on his own.

stunner-wrom

After the officer has taken his leave of us with a simply spoken, "'Day, now," and Bob has helped launch the kite down by the pond, where its crimson tail flutters vibrant in the thermal breeze, and after both mother and daughter have taken Bob's home phone number, promising to call and return the borrowed bandana, we walk the short distance back to my apartment. A plain brown-paper-wrapped package with an "Adam & Eve" return address waits outside my door, a post-it note attached to it declaring that, though we've yet to meet, the occupant of the apartment next door did me a favor and let in the UPS delivery person, thinking it the neighborly thing to do. "Knock on my door anytime," my neighbor concludes, "and have fun!"

"Thank you," I write at the bottom of the note and affix it to my neighbor's door without knocking. All things in good time.

"This is it," Bob says excitedly, depositing package on galley kitchen countertop and beginning to rip wrapping. He stops. "Mind if I have a little privacy? Take a nice long shower or something," he suggests. "Relax a little. It's been a big day for you. I can't believe that kite babe's actually gonna *call* me! Hey, her mother's pretty cute too. Maybe we could double date."

"Chances are she's married."

"Chances are she's married, divorced, married, and divorced again. I saw the look she gave you."

"The look of abject pity?"

Bob shrugs. "You gotta start *some*where."

"I'm past all that now," I say. "My priorities have been reprioritized."

"Mine too. Priority number one right now is getting laid."

"Please. Unseemly. The act of sexual congress should be a beautiful, spiritual, heartfelt thing."

"I know all that," Bob says, wagging his head tiredly. "My mom gave me the big sex lecture last year. She said when I discovered girls, I'd want to do certain fun and dirty things with them. 'But remember one thing,' she told me. 'Strive always to comport yourself with a girl in such a way that when they eventually film her autobiography, your small part in it isn't credited as Asshole #1.' Take a shower, Bob. I got work to do."

I decide instead to take a long, lingering bath, no easy task considering the cramped quarters of my tub and the ungainly length of my frame. Still, I manage to relax, to doze off even. I dream of signs, symbols, portents, an endless string of fuzzy abstractions, all whirling in orbit around an invisible black hole, all blissfully uncrunched.

I awaken immersed in cold water, chin lolling on knobby knees.

"You turning into a prune in there, Bob?" Bob calls through the door. "I'm almost set out here."

I towel myself dry, dress, and exit the bathroom. Bob squats behind the computer, hooking a wire from my telephone jack to the lowest tier of gadgetry.

"What's that for?"

"Modem," he answers, tongue between teeth in concentration. "Most of your neural net's back at my place. Don't worry, I got everything macroed in. You'll be connected automatically soon as you boot up. Just hit this switch here," he says, indicating a toggle on the front of what's left of the computer's chassis, "and you're in business." He stands, claps his hands together, performs a sort of bent-elbowed, fist-pumping, robotic two-step dance of triumph. "I can't believe it's finally ready," he says. "This thing is *so* cool!"

I can't help noticing the new addition to the apparatus. Suction-cupped to the vinyl seat of my swivel chair, a long and narrow cylindrical protuberance, angling slightly forward from the shaft, stands at attention, its bulbous, nubby tip covered with a fur of cilia-fine filaments. I touch it with a fingertip, marveling at its softness, and the flexible latex shaft bends and springs back. A bundle of multi-colored wires lead from cupped base to joystick on table in front of monitor.

"What's this for?" I ask.

Bob smiles. "Innernet communications," he says.

I lower my eyelids suspiciously. "Where does it go?"

"Uh, um." Bob clears his throat. "That'd have to be up the butt, Bob."

"Excuse me?"

"Up the rectum, Bob. It's your basic anally insertable signal receptor."

"Preposterous!" I say.

"I know, that's what *I* thought when I saw it in my dad's Adam & Eve catalogue (little Ma & Pa operation outa Carrboro, North Carolina that caters to the sexually stymied, is my guess). I'm like, 'You mean people use this for *fun?*' But the catalogue copy says that 'The Love Wand' (tee-hee) can be used for 'prostate stimulation,' which, if you've ever had a prostate exam, which I'm guessing you have, a man your age—you *have* had a prostate exam, haven't you Bob?"

"Yes, but—"

"How'd it turn out?"

"Benign enlargement. The physician suggested a wait-and-see approach."

"Good. Then you know the anal sphincter ain't necessarily an Exit-Only door, so easing this baby up the old fundament ain't preposterous at all. In fact, with a generous glob of good old 'Butter-Up'—which, I gotta say, I never truly appreciated the word 'viscous' till I squeezed out an experimental blob of, in a clinically controlled environment, of course—the procedure turns out to be *plenty* posterous."

"No."

"Really. Course I had to take out the vibrator mechanism to make room for the relay transistors—"

"No, no, no, no, no," I say. "What in the world can you be thinking of?"

"That'd be, 'Of what in the world can you—'"

"Enough!" I thunder. "Explain yourself, young man!"

"I was getting to that," Bob says, sulking. "You don't have to *yell* all over me."

"Sorry."

"It's OK," he says. "I can understand. Where to start?" he muses. "First of all, I guess I should tell you I was wrong about that Cloister-ROM thing."

"I should say."

"Not *all* wrong," Bob says, "but we gotta forget the hemispheric brain for a second. That's got nothing to do with anything. The more I thought about it, the more I realized that the kind of self-validating call you're waiting for still needs to be sent from an inner source to the brain, but it's not the brain that's sending the message."

"What's sending the message?"

Bob's face turns deadly serious. "Your soul, Bob."

"My soul?"

"That immutable, eternal part of you that is truly, like, *you*," he says.

"Assuming that I have one."

"Yeah, assuming, but that's not exactly a leap-of-faith assumption, Bob. Most scientists believe there's a soul, all right—talk to a sub-atomic quantum theorist if you don't believe me—but the main question is, *where?* So I did some research." He cocks his head jauntily, smiles at his own precocity. "Did you know that no fewer than thirty-three extant aboriginal tribes believe that the soul resides somewhere in the lower digestive tract, Bob? And these are tribes that have no knowledge of each other's existence! Coincidence, Bob? Where do you think all these separate peoples would get such an idea?"

"Dysentery?"

"Ha-ha, Bob. You're getting to be a very funny Bob lately. So I did a little more research. At first I wasted a lot of time on the appendix, thinking, 'Shit, it ain't good for much *else*, maybe *that's* where the soul is.' But I nixed that idea, ditto the whole small intestine (too far a stretch, your ilea and your jejunum, and don't even *mention* all those messy looking villi: what kind of soul would want to hang out *there?*). Moved my way past the cecum, took a left at the transverse colon (no luck), waved so long to the spleen in passing (no interchange to get off on anyway), and, at the splenic flexure (don't give me that look, Bob, I ain't making this shit up, you know) headed due south down the descending colon, feeling pretty hopeless at this point, I don't mind telling you." Bob's eyes light up suddenly. "Then I saw it. A cozy little S-curve in the road ahead. A safe and snug little loopy harbor for the soul to slip its ship in. Your sigmoid colon, Bob. I'm ninety-nine-point-nine-nine-nine percent positive that's where your soul is."

I look at the Love Wand, look back at Bob.

"Well, it's a *lot* more complicated than *that*, but who's got time to bore you with the details? Trust me, it's no coincidence that *soul* and *sigmoid* both begin with the letter *S*."

I frown.

"I know what you're thinking," he says, "but I didn't exactly *lie* to you about this Stunner thing, Bob. I just reserved some of the truth. Truth is, it stands for Sigmoidal Transmission Uploaded through Neural Net for, um, Electroencephalographic Reception."

I raise my eyebrows.

"It's just x-rays, Bob. You've had x-rays before, haven't you? Well, x-rays can carry units of info the neural net translates from sigmoidal transmission just as well as an electric current or even a microwave can. *Better* even."

I slowly shake my head.

"Don't call me crazy again, Bob, whatever you do."

"I'm not calling you crazy. It's just that none of this seems particularly real to me."

"Real!" Bob barks. "What do you know about reality?"

"It simply seems rather invasive," I say, "not to mention potentially dangerous."

"People get x-rays every day. People get sigmoidoscopies left and right. You telling me you never considered one, Bob, a man your age?"

"No."

"You ought to. Colon cancer's a major killer. Sigmoidoscopy's a walk in the park. *Dangerous*," Bob scoffs, laughing bitterly. "You're looking at the wrong ends of the word 'Stunner' if you want to talk *dang*erous."

"Meaning?"

Bob suddenly finds his sneakers interesting. He watches the toe of one scuff against the carpet. "I was gonna tell you," he says. "I wasn't gonna trick you into anything. Your Stunner is a complex machine, Bob. This ain't a ruby slipper thing. You don't just stick one end of a wire up your ass, stick the other end in your ear, hit the juice and say 'Gimme a call!' We ain't in Kansas anymore, Bob. This is science." He rubs his eyes wearily. It's been a long day for him. "You can't just loop your message from sigmoidal soul to brain," he goes on carefully. "Soul and brain are *already* looped by the whole nervous system. The message, like I said before, is being sent continuously, so continuously that, in effect, it goes without saying. There's nothing new about it, so you don't even recognize it as a message. It's like breathing or the heart beating or (closer yet!) cell division—it's going on all the time but you aren't really aware of it. So my idea is to splice into the loop again, only this time we use a machine that can receive, learn, and *interpret* the message, so it'll look all fresh and new and your brain can recognize it as something new and thus be made *aware* of it. Only problem is, in order to enable the neural net to interpret and transmit that message, I had to give it write permissions."

"Meaning?"

"There's a silent *W* in front of your ROM. The neural net can write on your brain."

"And that's dangerous? I remember your twin brother mentioning something about that."

"Um, yeah. It's *tricky*, is what it is, Bob. You gotta be careful, is all. See, the neural net can receive, learn, and interpret, but it's not really human. It can't feel fear."

"And what should it fear, Bob?"

Bob raises his eyebrows, shakes his head. "I don't know. Maybe whatever it is your *brain* fears. What if the *real* reason your brain isn't acknowledging your soul's message is it doesn't like the message?"

"Come again?"

"Well, what if the message isn't 'I'm me! Who're you?' I mean, who *knows* what the soul has to tell us, Bob? Who knows what your average soul wants? Freedom from flesh, maybe? The freedom to energize and just soar up into the sun? What if the soul's message is 'Lemme *outa* here, I wanna *fly!*' What if the neural net takes that message, learns it, and translates it into the kind of logic your brain can understand? I'm afraid the only logical translation of a message like that would be, 'Kill yourself, ASAP,' and since the neural net has write permissions, if it transmits that message, your brain would read it as its own executive decision." Bob purses his lips thoughtfully, shivers suddenly. "We're talking a slightly iffy situation here, Bob."

"Are you telling me that you were going to hook me up to a machine that might make me want to kill myself just to release my soul?"

"I *told* you I was going to tell you about it first. And I just did. We're talking *hypothetical* iffy situation, Bob. Your soul's message could be, 'Hey, cutie, how's it hanging?' for all I know. Plus anyway, I took a precaution." He reaches into his pocket, pulls out a foil packet the size of a fingernail. "I whipped up this little batch of lysergic acid (diethylamide, doncha know, which I can't believe how *easy* the recipe is). Take this about twenty minutes before you boot up, you'll be tripping so good, it should tone down the effects of any undesirable message from your soul. You get a message that tells you to kill yourself, your brain'll interpret it as a bad trip and ride it out. You get happy-go-lucky greetings from your soul, your brain'll get this dopey grin on its face and go, 'Cool.' Either way, you oughta be safe. Either way, you get your message."

I stand stunned.

"So it's decision time, Bob. The technology's waiting and here you are stalling. I mean, *you're* the one who wanted this crazy call in the first place."

"Perhaps."

"What're you saying, Bob? You want the call or what?"

I take a moment to consider this. It's been a long, long day for me as well, and I can find no place to rest. "I don't really think I'm waiting for that call any longer," I say, after a time. "I think perhaps I'm really waiting for something else."

Bob stares at me, open-mouthed. "Like what?"

"I don't know," I answer honestly.

"Great," Bob spits out. "That's just great. I start a project, I work my ass off on it, I'm *this* close to wrapping the whole thing up, and you change the specs on me. Why don't people like working with geniuses? Gimme one good reason, Bob."

"Because genius is too often misunderstood?"

"You said it," Bob says, and suddenly he begins to cry.

"What's the matter?" I say, shocked at his emotion.

"It's so useless, man," he weeps. "It's *all* iffy. It's all *guess*work. It *sounds* good. It makes every bit of logical sense in the *world*. I'm ninety-nine-point-nine-nine-nine percent positive, but that other point-oh-oh-one percent's killing me. I'm short of the event horizon, Bob. I don't know *anything* for sure. I may as *well* be crazy!"

And at that, Bob leans over my galley kitchen countertop, buries his face in his hands, and, shoulders shaking, breath hiccupping, sobs like a child denied.

"There, there," I say, leaning over him, my hand on his trembling back. I feel the heat of his frustration rising through his t-shirt. I stroke the back of his flushed and stubbly head. "There, there," I say again, the meaningless words soothing our misery like a mantra.

Epi-lude

Early the next morning, my intercom buzzes.

"Mr. Roberts?" a baritone voice says.

"Yes?"

"It's Ethan's parents. Let us in."

"Ethan?" I say.

I hear a female voice whispering in the background.

"Also known as Bob," he says with crisp resignation.

I buzz them up.

"We don't have much time," the dapper-looking man says, still standing in my doorway though his wife has entered before him and stands coolly appraising my abode. "We tried calling last night, but your phone seems to be out of order." He glances at his watch. "I have a breakfast meeting, and my wife's schedule is similarly booked, though, as you can clearly see, she was much too upset to put this off any longer."

I turn her way. Dressed in gray blazer and matching skirt, dark hair done up in neat bun, she appears to be relatively calm. Neither smiling nor frowning, she meets my gaze. "Is this yours?" she says, waving a hand to encompass my work station, my apartment, my life.

"Yes."

"And this?" she says, bending to flick a fingertip at the head of Bob's sigmoidal transmitter. Its shaft bends and springs, wiggles obscenely. She recoils, removes hankie from blazer pocket, assiduously wipes her hands with it.

"Let me explain," I begin.

"I can't imagine," the woman interrupts, "what kind of explanation we'd care to hear from you." Her eyes narrow darkly. "But perhaps I should explain something to *you*, Mr. Roberts (if that is, indeed, your real name). I returned home from work yesterday to find a credit card bill in the mail that listed a purchase from a certain sexual storefront, a purchase I never made or authorized. I called the credit card company to clear up the mistake and discovered that the purchase had indeed been made on my card for something called—" she allows herself a shudder of revulsion here "—a 'love wand.' Suffice to say that after I confronted Ethan with proof of the purchase (after questioning and clearing my husband, sorry *again*, dear), he admitted to having made the purchase himself and, upon further questioning, confessed that he's been 'spending some time' over here lately, working on a certain 'experiment.'"

"It's true that he's been here," I say, "but I can assure you that—"

"You can give your assurances to the police, Mr. Roberts," the man interrupts. "We notified them this morning, just after we fired the babysitter, and *we've* been assured that they will act on our complaint, just as soon as they can assign an officer to the case."

"Our son is a gifted and sensitive child," the woman says, "so we would appreciate it if, once charged, you would simply plead nolo contendere and spare Ethan the embarrassment of courtroom testimony. That is, of course, your decision to make."

"But if you don't make that decision," the man says, "we are prepared to exert every method of pressure at our disposal, up to and including hiring a paid professional persuader, to persuade you to make the proper decision. Our son is a gifted yet emotionally vulnerable child, and when we think of the sorts of vile 'experiments' you've subjected him to here in this awful place—" a sob escapes him "—under the ruse of your so-called 'scientific method,' well, let me simply point out that we would protect him from any further abuses with our checkbook and your very life. I'd like to kill you right now, if I could."

"We'd both like to kill you right now," the woman says, "though we doubt you'd ever agree to that. Our son is a gifted and extremely troubled child who, even as we speak, is nearly frantic with misdirected fury, throwing a tantrum behind the door of his locked room and swearing that he'll build a duplicate of this—" she sniffs in disgust, negligently indicates the sigmoidal transmitter with wave of hand "—this *machine* and finish your so-called 'experiment' all on his own."

Both man and woman close their eyes, shudder in unison.

"The key clause," the man says, "that we wish you to understand here today, is that our son is a *child*—gifted, troubled, loving, maddening, innocent, emotionally unstable, intelligent, disingenuous, the list could go on and on," he finishes breathlessly. "But Ethan is a *child*, after all, *our* child, and you, sir, are an *adult*. There are strict laws that apply. You won't be seeing Ethan anymore, Mr. Roberts (assuming the rather dubious veracity of that name), and neither will you be seeing us."

"You will, however," the woman finishes, "be seeing the police, our attorneys, and whatever other paid consultants prove necessary to bring this sordid story to a hastened yet satisfying conclusion."

"Good day," they both say, and they walk out my door.

•

Before the police eventually arrive, I decide to 'drop' the 'LSD' Bob has left for me. If anyone deserves to be a guinea pig in this 'sordid story,' that someone is me. I open the foil to discover a single square blotter the size of my pinkie fingernail upon which Bob—or is it 'Ethan' now?—has penciled a crude face :) smiling innocently up at me. I return the smile, deposit blotter on tongue, swallow. Its flavor neither pleases nor dis-. While waiting for the LSD to 'kick in,' I write a brief note to Bob, explaining that since I value our friendship dearly, I cannot stand the thought of him risking both mind and life conducting an experiment upon himself that could be of no earthly value to him, since it was never he who awaited what I now can only consider to be a fictitious call in the first place. "Study the results," I write. "Learn," I write on. "But find your *own* call to answer. Your friend," I conclude, "Bob."

I fold and seal the note in an envelope, scrawl "BOB" across the front in great block capitals (with "a.k.a. Ethan" cursived beneath, just in case), and tuck it amid the short-circuited effluvia of his toolbox, hoping beyond hope that, should something happen to me, the police will eventually deliver it.

I strip off my clothes, stand pale and awkward before my work station, and, catching wispy trails of color on the periphery of my vision that signal the time is ripe, lube up with a healthy handful of "Butter-Up" and carefully lower my squatting bulk onto the business end of the sigmoidal love wand.

I endeavor to relax.

The less said the better.

Mission mortifyingly accomplished, I fasten the Velcro strap across my chest, don welder's mask, and, effectively blinded now, fumble for joystick and toggle. Locating the former, I rest its base in my lap, grip it firmly (heh-heh); locating the latter, I flip it on.

Computer hums.

Nothing.

I squirm uncomfortably, diddle with joystick experimentally.

Nothing.

"There, there," I say aloud. "It's nothing, really."

Nothing.

I close my eyes within the darkness of my mask.

Something?

There is a pinprick of light in the distance. I push forward on the joystick, and the pinprick gradually grows to orb. I push forward further and orb grows to luminescent sphere, rushing toward me until it completely fills the screen of my vision. I hear a ringing in the distance just as I discover a pinprick of darkness piercing the light. The darkness grows, becomes visible, rushes toward me, orb, sphere, all encompassing world of utter darkness and suddenly the rushing stops and I am floating above/below/in orbit around the hole.

There is a faint ringing.

I float here now forever it seems, weightless, bodiless, wantless—an enticingly tantalizing whisper of deja vu stretching out above/below me just barely out of reach—when suddenly off to my right in the dark hole's corona of whirling brightness, I espy two amorphous blobs of hyperplasm, mirror images of one another, rotating slowly but surely, counter- and clockwise, connected by a single infinitesimally linear strand of pure energy.

"What are they doing, Bob?" a voice whispers in my ear.

"Waiting," I say, and I know that it's true.

"Don't talk outa your ass, Bob (heh-heh). I got one word for you."

I don't ask. I have no need to.

"Synergy, Bob. That's what these Bob-blobs have, it's clear to see." There is a soft chuckle. "What do you suppose *we* look like to *them*?"

"We?" I say.

"Don't backslide, Bob. It's unseemly."

Silence.

"Feel like a hand of gin rummy, maybe, to pass the time?"

"No."

Silence. An con's worth. A thinly whistled off-key tune. "Man, Bob, when you hallucinate, you really hallucinate."

Silence. A distant ringing.

"Want me to get that?"

"It doesn't matter."

Silence.

"Well, you got more patience than *I* do," the voice says. "I gotta split before I die of boredom."

"You can do that?"

"Fuck yeah," the voice says, "excuse my singular diction. I can fly off whenever I want to. Can't you?"

"I don't know."

"Well, it's been fun," the voice says. "If I don't see you in the future, I'll see you in the pasture."

"Wait," I say. "Um."

"Yes?"

"I'll miss you," I say.

"But I'll miss you most of all. (Oops! Think those Bob-blobs heard me? Wouldn't want to hurt their feelings.) Plus hey! Before I go, what do you think would've happened if Dorothy *caught* her balloon ride with the wizard? Where do you think he would've taken her?"

"I don't know. Where?"

"Sure as hell not back to fucking *Kan*sas, Bob."

And suddenly a streak of light from behind me arcs up and outward, loops gracefully across the horizon, and zeros in on the hole below, exploding in a flash of utter black.

There is a ringing in my ears. Someone stands above me, my welder's mask in his big hands. Light glints from his badge.

"Hello," he says.

"Hello," I say.

"Shush," he says when I try to rise, and his big hands push me back. "Wait'll the paramedics get here. This thing's *gotta* hurt," he says. "My advice: watch where you sit from now on."

I focus on his beaten face, the scarred eyebrow, the crooked smile.

"My wife'll never believe this when I tell her," he says.

"*You*," I say, too weak to resist.

He laughs, face lighting up radiant as the sun, and he places a calloused hand on my brow. "You were expecting?"

Take me. Take me, I say. I'm ready now.

About the Author

Pat Rushin is the author of the story collection *Puzzling Through the News*. His original feature-length screenplay, *The Zero Theorem*, was produced in 2014 by The Zanuck Company and Voltage Pictures, and directed by Terry Gilliam. He has published essays, screenplays, and poetry, but mostly stories, in a variety of literary magazines, including *The North American Review*, *Quarterly West*, *Sudden Fiction*, *Indiana Review*, *The Beloit Poetry Journal*, *The Johns Hopkins Magazine*, *American Literary Review*, *Fwriction:Review*, and elsewhere. He teaches creative writing at the University of Central Florida, where he has also (twice upon a time) served as editor of *The Florida Review*.

www.ingramcontent.com/pod-product-compliance
Lightning Source LLC
Chambersburg PA
CBHW030645190726
48286CB00008B/2674